STORIES
IN THE WORST
WAY

GARY LUTZ

With gratitude to Derek White.

ISBN-13: 978-0-9798080-7-4
ISBN-10: 0-9798080-7-3

First Calamari Press edition, 2009
First 3rd bed paperback edition, 2002
First Alfred A. Knopf, Inc., cloth edition, 1996

Cover by Derek White.

Published by Calamari Press, Nairobi/Detroit

www.calamaripress.com

For Gordon Lish

CONTENTS

SORORALLY

What could be worse than having to be seen resorting to your own life? In my case, there was a fixed sum of experiences, of people, to or from which I could not yet add or subtract, but which I was skilled at coming to grief over, crucially, in broad daylight. For instance, not too long ago I concerned one of the local women, a fruitful botch of a girl. We worked side by side—did data-entry and look-up, first shift, in an uncarpeted, unair-conditioned recess of the ground floor of a bricky low-rise. I was forever taking her in over the partition of bindered reference directories that bisected our workstation. I would keep a sidelong watch over her as she ordered her daily allowance of cough drops in echelon on a square of paper towel. May the arms of other people be said to have an atmosphere? At the very least, may they be construed as aromatic systems of bone and down? Hers enjoyed, for my sake alone, an intimate publicity above the little dove-gray squares of her keyboard.

And the pastime she had! You are familiar, at least, with those bubble packs that almost everything gets sold in nowadays? She used to peel the clear plastic bubble away from its anchoring cardboard, emancipate what she had bought (yet another handset cord for her

7

phone, maybe, or another pencil sharpener, or one of those tricky tooth-whitening sets), then stow into the bubble whatever she happened to have at hand (blood-gaudied parabolas of dental floss; some saxophone-shaped lengths of black plastic that paired socks had hung from in stores; significant clothespins; muculent tissues), reaffix the bubble to the cardboard base, then post the culled, reliquary results on one of the cork tiles that lined the wall of a corridor, where everybody, including me alone, could not help having to see.

Our days, it turned out, held a lot of the same things. Mornings would arrive piecemeal, filling themselves out little by little, summoning tiny inheritances from the previous day—memorial resources in the form, say, of dust suddenly abundant enough for us to thumb from our screens—until there were valid hours bearing us up and we could at last swoon away from our machines.

My eyes would chance ambitiously onto hers.

The woman possessed an appropriately full, planet-like face. It had things on it I always took for something else—on her chin, for instance, a bluish streaklet that I assumed had to be ink. A bungled complexion, in short, and teeming features.

Inquiry: at what point do people become environments for one another to enter? I was entertaining thoughts along these lines because I had only recently brought to an end a period of clandestine gender on my part, a period of not having allowed my life to register on any part of me that saw the light of day. I had now gone as far as collaborating with my body to raise a pivotal tilde of a mustache.

One night, after work, under the ribbed dome of my umbrella (the one torn panel fixed over the back of my head), I thus led her to a restaurant. We perspired baffledly over our deep soups and did not look each other in the eye at first. I think I gulped around my food without eating very much of it. (I have been told that I swallow air.) I eventually started in on her, tendering the usual explanation—that people banded together into little domestic populations and could be seen getting up, *en bloc*, from tables.

I went on to be understood that I did not expect to ever be cooked for, but that I would probably never stop expecting to smell cooking. I brought my parents into it, too—how I was their descendant, someone who had come down from not too high a height; how I had one foot in the two of them; how in my reflection in the greensick screen of my monitor I could sometimes make out a riling rehash of their faces; how they were no doubt speaking right that very moment at the top of my current voice.

For her part, she told me that as a schoolgirl she had been dismissed late one morning with sticklets of charcoal and clunches of unruled paper, and had been instructed not to come back until she had made rubbings of what it was like where she lived: the fretwork along the upper walls, the nailheads and knots of the floorboards, every unevenness of her household. Always pegging away at some fitting trouble, she said. People were always either coming into money or going through her things.

She paid out her arms toward me so slowly, so concealedly, across the tabletop as she spoke that I did not notice until her fingers had closed around my wrists.

Then her room: an unsociable half-circle of folding chairs. One of those collapsible music stands erect on its tripod—the lyrelike shelf, where the music was supposed to sit, holding out an open telephone directory instead. A sink and a splishing faucet and stacks of hand towels, face towels, bath towels, washcloths. No bed, just some mats we had to uncurl. The lamp made a tinny, frustrated sound when I switched it off. I imagine I must have unbundled her, peeled off her underdressings, dipped my fingers into her, sopped and woggled them around, browsing, *consulting* what she had made of herself inside.

Afterward: sink wash, sponge baths.

Because some days the world holds true at the drop of a hat, don't you find? Things favor themselves: whatever you reach for—a shimmered arm, or parts unknown—is ready, finally, to have itself handled. Other days, you can barely exempt yourself from what you might still be capable of. Instead of sleep, the most you count on getting is some cheesy quiet. It follows, then—should it not?—that in even the thinnest of light there are places at which to come to an accurate parting of the ways. At the most, I may have broken something not too major or prominent of hers.

In due time, though, I had her on the phone.

"Sororally," she was saying. "As a sister."

She walked off the job, or got herself promoted, reassigned, not long after that. I took it in my head to go back to the restaurant just once. I brought along a plump, companionable section of the *Courier-Tribune*—the part with the unremitting regional spot news. Swivel-eyed eaters took me in as I picked my way to the booth. How much harm could I have meant? A woman sat down, unaccompanied, to peer at me from the next booth—a much older woman, a differently futile ensemble of smells and noisings. I remember that during the progress of the meal (I had ordered one of the big, busying specials), I disturbed the pages of my newspaper, spoiling them, melancholizing them with sudden prosperities of eyesight, despecificating the stories until all that was still binding in them was a vague and ungiving sense of people motioning dimly toward me from within their own cumbersome towns.

I left off my reading and brought the paper down a final time, then stared ahead at the woman, with the news, and all I had done to it, still on view in my eyes. I exacted it onto her—*confirmed* it. This was as much as it took to get her up and going, her body irked forward by its clique of meddling organs. For my part, I must have made a decision to see how much of the ink I could soap off my hands.

To get into the men's room, you went through a door and immediately—no more than two feet in— discovered a second door, heavier, unpainted; and before you could get the thing open, you had to make room by reopening, by a good half-foot, the one you had already pushed through.

WAKING HOURS

Three hours after I quit my telemarketing job, I got hired to teach middle-level managers how to bestow awards on undeserving employees. I would run through the presentation on a Monday, say, and then early the next day—when I'd more than likely still be portaging things back from sleep—I would get a call to hurry down and repeat the performance for the same group of people. That would usually lead to a two- or three-week booking at the same outfit and for the same bruised-looking men and women, who eventually got the picture and passed the quizzes, which, admittedly, were hard.

I was in receipt of the mothered-down version of the kid every other Saturday. The bus would make an unscheduled stop in front of the building where I lived, and then out he would come, morseled in an oversized down jacket, all candy-breathed from the ride. I would drive us to a family restaurant where we would slot into seats opposite each other and he would ask me the questions his mother had asked him to ask. I had a quick-acting, pesticidal answer for every one.

When the food arrived—kiddie-menu concentrates for him, an overproportioned hamburger for me—I would tilt the conversation toward him, maybe a little too steeply. I would want to poach on the life inside him, whatever it was. He would splay his hands on the tabletop, arms slat-straight, crutching himself up.

After lunch, in the undemanding dark of a movie theater where he goggled at some stabby, Roman-numeraled sequel, I would plug my ears and loot my own heart.

I lived in an apartment, defined as a state or condition of being apart. My life was cartoned off in three rooms and bath, one of several dozen lives banked above a side street. I convinced myself that there were hours midway through the night when the walls slurred over and became membranes, allowing seepages and exchanges from unit to unit; hours when the tenants, all asleep except me, dispersed themselves into the air and mixed themselves with their neighbors. This at least accounted for dreams that rarely jibed with experiences.

One night, I posted myself at the city's only gay bar that catered to older, self-devastated types. I lapped at a Coke until I got picked out by a drizzly blond—mid-thirties, lightly muscled arms thinning out of his too-short sleeves. He conducted me through a snarl of alleys to his apartment. It was small and airless and hassocky. He was blond everywhere except his crotch, where the wreath of hairs was cola-colored and looked barbered, fussed over. I let him slant himself inside me. My thoughts arrowed from the general to the particular: a kid, an emotionable bad apple, whom I'd sat across from in high-school Honors World Cultures, hounded by his girlishly cursive arms.

I felt something.

I caked some words over what I'd felt.

Days got pocked with facts, names, sights. I was given an office of my own with the understanding that there was no promotion involved, just the freeing up of space. I rewrote my presentations. I lunched at a diner where the paper placemats had been designed to divert bored kids. I always had several pens with me, but they stayed in my pocket. Except once. Once I connected some dots.

Nights were slopwork.

After work, I wasn't above ducking into a large supermarket and picking up five or six items almost at random, then approaching the long row of checkout lanes and skimming the faces of the men working the registers (women were disqualified) until I found one who looked as if he'd had a little too much to live, one who would lavish on my purchases and my implied need for them the most generous interpretation possible. I would choose his aisle. I would get in line. When it was my turn, when he was ringing up my items, we would be close in spirit. I would dizzy him with eye contact. Everything—my life—would be riding on what he would say, on the certainty that he would say something.

The kind of reading I was doing involved pushing the words around on the page, trying to bully them into doing what I wanted them to do. What I wanted them to do was tell me what to say when the phone rang at night and the unfamiliar, expectant, undebauched womanly voice of the misdialing caller asked, "Who is this?"

For the better part of a week, I was ashamed of myself for having refused to participate in a simple little educational exercise the first time I was asked. On a downtown street during my lunch-hour half-hour, a kid had come up to me—a kid with an oily scrub of beard and a clipboard—and said: "I'm supposed to tell ten people what I stand for and then get each to sign this piece of paper. They won't let me back into class until I get ten people."

He had waved the clipboard at me. I'd seen six or seven fake-looking signatures on a piece of steno-book paper.

I kept walking. I'd already known what this kid stood for: animal rights, beer by the keg, all you can eat, perpetual calendars at the back of telephone directories, sadomasochism that had real caring behind it, the right to Xerox whatever you pleased.

"Thanks a lot," he called out as I kept on walking.

On the next block, I was approached by a Puerto Rican woman who told me she stood for unity and excitement. She shoved her clipboard at me. I signed a name.

Some nights the saddest I got was when a street stopped. In a medium-sized city like that, they all did, eventually—guttering out into roads, flanging out into highways, dead-ending, slamming perpendicularly into boulevards and then never picking up their thread again. When a street stopped, I would want out-of-town papers, the advertising supplements of faraway department stores. I would want to know what the people living in those cities could get that I couldn't get in my city.

I got used to being one of sleep's discards.

I would find myself pushed out, fully clothed, onto my new bedspread, which did not deliver on the promise of *spread*, which did not offer anything in the way of vistas, prospects. Next to me, on the floor, still untrashed, would be the plastic bag the bedspread had come in. It read: "CAUTION: THIS BAG IS NOT A TOY." I kept it there to remind me that everything was in lieu of everything else.

A Saturday, my kid again: my follow-through, my finish line, a livelong shape I'd kinked out of a woman when I could tell their faces apart—when women, womankind, seemed divisible into units, each unit customized with individuating gimmicks and specialties. In this case, the woman, if memory serves, was a well-thumbed, uninhabitable redhead, a health-care provider.

My ex-wife: I could tell that a lot of thought had gone into the things she had taken out on me.

In addition to the wife, I'd had parents. They were the people who had told me, the day I turned seven, that I was old enough to order my own ice-cream cone. They were seated on a bench on the boardwalk overlooking the sand and the beach umbrellas. I was wearing the brace that the doctors had put on the wrong part of me. Pinching a quarter, I wheeled around and squeaked over to the line of concession stands. A voice came out and ordered a cone.

The lady behind the counter said, "No such thing."

I guess I had a look on my face—a disturbance—that made her keep going. "I'm only orangeade, *she's* custard," she said, pointing across the partition—a

16

clumsily nailed plank—to the lady at the next stand. The two ladies shared the same low ceiling.

The afternoon was glassy and overdetailed.

Meaning what? That I grew up on the spot? That years later it would take great effort and willpower to wave away the first available thumby, unsucked dick and wait instead—in line, if need be—for some cunted, varicosed smashup on which to hazard my desolating carnality?

Most nights, I was not so much living my life as roughing out loose, galling paraphrases of the lives being lived in the adjoining apartments and hallways. Someone would make a move (clear his throat, probably, or flush a toilet), and, after a reasonable minute, I would do something that approximated it (scrape a kitchen chair across linoleum, no doubt), something that in the end amounted to the same thing. I developed a vast overdependence on my sources, my fellow tenants, whom I went out of my way to avoid meeting because I hated them for beating me to what my life boiled down to.

Street Map of the Continent

Some days his work took him into people's houses. He would enter a room, part the air, odor things differently, then come out with whatever it was. Never a word of thanks from anybody, but he would usually get asked if he needed to use the bathroom—a powder room, more often than not. He would picture the owners listening to the flushes, counting.

He lived with a woman who volunteered at the library and brought a different book home with her every night. She would sit with it open on her lap and work the tip of an uncrooked paper clip into the gutter where the facing pages met, prying things loose: fingernail peelings, eyebrow hairs, pickings and outbursts and face-scrapings. Anything on the plane of the page itself—the immediate, heedless presence of the previous reader in the form of abundances of shed hair, perhaps, or gray powderings of scalp—she swept onto the floor. She evacuated the book, then ran the vacuum cleaner. In the morning, the book went back to the library.

The man had his own chair and watched her like a hawk.

There were a few years of cordial intimacy with the woman, and then her teeth began to lose their way in her gums. They listed and slid. The sticky hair she had always combed into a canopy over her forehead started to droop, and the color went dim. Her eyes seemed to take him in less and less.

One morning she was nowhere the man could see. Most of the clothes she had liked were gone, too.

He called in sick.

He sat in his chair, watching the kitchen from the hour when the table was a breakfast table to the hour when it was a supper table.

He started buying newspapers—anything he could get his hands on, one of each. There were some papers that came out only once a week and printed the menus of the senior-citizen high-rises in town. The man tore out the menus and taped them to the refrigerator door as ideas, suggestions.

The grocery store where he bought the papers was not part of a chain. The floor dipped and sloped. The aisles started out as ample causeways, veered off, then narrowed down to practically nothing. There were vitrines back there. Display cases. Nobody seemed particular about what went into them. The man started bringing things to add.

Her shoes, with the gloating, mouthy look that shoes acquire when no longer occupied.

Her stockings, riveled and unpleasant to touch.

Sheet after sheet of her sinking penmanship.

Numbers, calculations, she had steepened onto graph paper.

One night, he called the home number of the man who lined up the jobs for him.

"Yes," the voice said, over TV noise.

He put the phone down. Her smoking and sewing tackle were on the telephone stand. He put them in a bag to take to the store.

The sleeplessness spread to his arms and his legs. He practiced removing her absence from one place and parking it somewhere else. There was too much furniture in the house, he decided.

The town was one whose name the citizens had never had to spell out on the envelope when paying a bill or sending a card locally. Instead, they could just write *City*. Then came a generation who grew up suspecting there were two different places—one a town, the other a city—with the same sets of streets and addresses. These people were less sure of where they lived and spent too much time deciding whether the shadows that fell across sidewalks and playgrounds were either too big or too little for whatever the shadows were supposed to be shadows of. These were people who dreamed of towers that would never quite stay built even in dreams.

Depending on which authorities the man read, he could be counted as part of either generation.

The only other thing ever known about him was that when it came time to take his car in for the annual inspection, he sat in a little waiting area off to the side of the garage. A mechanic came in and told him that they had gone ahead and put a sticker on the car, but there were oral disclaimers about the brakes, the tires. "I don't know what kind of driving you do," the mechanic said. "Is it mostly around here, or highway?"

"Highway," the man said.

Weeks went by before he thought to stop.

Slops

Because I had colitis, I divided much of my between-class time among seventeen carefully chosen faculty restrooms, never following the same itinerary two days in a row, using a pocket notebook to keep track. I had to wear three thicknesses of underwear. By the end of a class day, my innermost briefs would be elaborately rimed, embrowned, impastoed.

Did I ever worry about the smell when I was passing out handouts in class? Because all I did was pass out handouts and read them out loud, then collect them and dismiss the class. None of it would be on the test. There were no tests—just papers. Not essays, themes, reviews, reports, compositions, critiques, research projects—but papers, sheets of paper, stapled together. I'd lightly pencil a grade in the upper right-hand corner, and that would be it—no comments or appraisals subjoined in authoritative swipes of a felt-tip pen. I made sure no telltale signs—spilled coffee, dog-ears, creases, crumples, crimps, fingerprint grime—would lead students to believe that their papers had ever been read. But I read them hard, expecting sentences to have been spitefully spatchcocked into the running gelatinization of barbarisms and typos to check up on me, to see if I was actually reading. For instance: "Dear 'Professor': You fucking stink. Try wiping yourself once and [sic] awhile [sic]. Or didn't they teach that were [sic] you went to school? Bag it." But I never found any such intertrudings.

I was midway through my shadowed, septic thirties. I had been hired as a generalist. What I taught was vague and interdisciplinary and unchallengeable. Whatever I said, it was bound to be correct up to a point. My credentials were fraudulent. I'd awelessly faked my way through a Midwestern graduate school with a dissertation two hundred and eighty-seven clawing, suffixy pages long, all of it embezzled from leaky monographs. Since then, I'd taught myself to mooch off nobody but myself.

After each class, I lumped my way to whichever men's room my notebook said was next. My life was an ambitious program of self-centrifugalization. I was casting myself out.

Three "once"s:

Once

Once, there was no way for me to get out of having lunch with a colleague. He had the beard, the paunch, the patter. We sat in the faculty dining room, where I had never eaten before and never afterward ate again. He recalled the previous day's special: "chicken cordon sanitaire, potatoes non grata, vegetable mêlée." He said that his profession involved "belaboring the oblivious." He talked about a diffident colleague of ours who, at department meetings, when given the floor, "bent down to wax it." He said that when the annual departmental picture was taken, the camera went "C-L-I-Q-U-E." I blinked and swallowed, hoisted smiles, poked at and beveled the block of beef on my plate. When he excused himself to rush off for a one-o'clock class, I sought out the dining-room men's room, one that wasn't on any of my regular campus tours. Unlike the nookish, single-person-occupancy arrangements I frequented (their hollow-board doors securing me from corridoral traffic only by the flimsy expedient of a hook and an eyebolt), this was a vast, modern affair with a line of urinals and three stalls. One of the latter was unoccupied, so, taking a seat, I busied myself with some noodling and valving, the virtually noiseless preliminaries, until, emboldened by the whoosh of a neighbor's flush and satisfied that it would muffle the report of my own bowels, I splattered myself out.

Once

Once, I attended a meeting of the university senate. Why? Because I had an urge to sit in a room with people, adults, salaried specialists. The day before, a sunless Sunday, I'd driven to a mall, where, from the remainder bin of a chain bookstore, I'd plucked a slim paperback by a doctor, a physician, that said the drizzled stools of a patient with colitis should be regarded as tears. So the next morning, I sat among a hundred or so of my colleagues and listened to a soon-to-retire administrator, a dean of some kind, say two things that I have not since been able to displace. One was that during his long career in the classroom he had learned many, many things from his students. I tried to think of one thing, anything, that I had ever learned from mine. Aside from the example of their grooming habits, sleeve-roll-up techniques, the novelties of their

23

wristwear, etc., I couldn't come up with anything. The other thing the administrator said was that we all needed to love our students, that in many cases these kids weren't getting enough, or any, love at home. In the men's room afterward, I thought about my students, the whole faceless, rostered population of them. I did not love them, did not feel a trace of affection for them, but did I hate them? I decided that it wasn't exactly hate.

ONCE

Once, for what must have been well over a month, a dog-eyed girl, a student, a young woman really, at least twenty-three, dimly recognizable from the front-row center of one of my classes, began stopping by for a few minutes during my office hours. She always had at least three questions Magic Markered on pastel-hued index cards, and she asked them in a dampened, worn-away voice. She was an Informational Sciences major. My course was an elective.

One day, after I had answered her questions by hanging, as usual, some suspect, oversyntaxed curtains of explanation in the air between us, she capped her pen and said, "You need a buddy." She wasn't smiling, she wasn't being sarcastic, she wasn't unsteadying me with a stare. Her eyes were a muddy brown. She had an oily cumulus of biscuit-colored hair. She was wearing a windbreaker, a box-pleated skirt, brown socks. There was an untended, blotchy loveliness about her that had my cock smarting.

I balanced the image of her along the rim of my mind in the men's room afterward during an especially boiling, bustling efflux, and it occurred to me: Did

24

people think I was beating off in there? Were people keeping track of the time? Had some busybody logged me in? I had the stink working in my favor, but how long after my exit would it be until somebody actually came in and registered the stink and related it to my occupancy?

When the girl showed up, uninvited but not unexpected, late one afternoon at the house I rented on a pinched street, I offered her dinner—a microwavable box of chicken. I put her at ease by standing in the kitchen and following the red digital countdown on the face of the microwave. She lotus-positioned herself on the living-room floor, started jerking through the classified section of the paper.

"I'm moving out," she said. Then: "My stepmom, my mother, my boyfriend, school, your class."

"Everything?" I said.

"All of it. Completely. Practically."

I arranged some napkins and forks on the coffee table.

"By the way, that smell," she said. "Now I know."

I watched her eat. I listened to her talk. Then I watched her lead the way to the bedroom.

Undressing myself, lowering myself into bed with someone new, I always reminded myself that whichever women had ever climbed on top of me before had actually just been laddering themselves up onto somebody else. About halfway through, maybe even sooner, they'd be absolutely sure of it. They'd know *who*. What was happening with this girl was this: I was handing her back to her boyfriend on a platter.

After she left, I grabbled around in my desk for my grade book, then slapped on bare feet toward the bathroom. Once seated, I turned to MWF 9:15–10:15,

25

Stevenson Hall 142A, and found her: Ramsey, Val. She'd been doing "A" work. In my course, "A" work meant turning in so many sheets of paper over so many weeks. Thirty sheets, fifteen weeks, I think.

There is actually a fourth "once," something I did that didn't involve taking a crampy, squdging shit afterward.

Once, on a table in the faculty lounge in the building where my office was, I found a rain-wrinkled newspaper open to the comics page. There was nobody else around. I took a pencil out of my inside pocket. In the white squares between the black ziggurats of the crossword puzzle, I penciled, in heavy, ham-handed caps untraceable to me: COULD EVERYBODY PLEASE BE A LITTLE LESS SPECIFIC? STARTING RIGHT NOW?

Devotions

From time to time I show up in myself just long enough for people to know they are not in the room alone. Usually, these are people who expect something from me—a near future, a not-too-distant future. What I tell them is limited to the people I have already had myself married against. Everything I say is to the best of my knowledge and next to nothing. It comes nowhere close.

My first wife, my blood wife, had no background to speak of, no backdrop of relations, customs, scenery. She arrived sharp-spined and already summed up. We ate out all the time and spoke lengthily, vocabularily, about whatever got set before us, especially the meat, with its dragged-out undersong of lifelong life. There was no end to the occasions on which the woman and I got along in public and in private. I remember a smell she had on just her arms, an endearment, something that she had been born with or that had traveled a great distance to land on her. I am almost certain that there was much more to what there was of us—I think we had a house, some coverings at the very least—but the night she gave me what was obviously a severance fuck, nothing needed to be said, nobody needed to be told off. I left right away. The time I looked back, the evidence was slight.

It was the second wife who drank. It was always up to me to cart her back and forth to work. The job titles she had during the time I was married to her could be listed either alphabetically or chronologically; I am not sure what difference, if any, such a list would make. But the addresses—we moved from house to house, although they were never houses per se, just blunt-roofed, boxlike constructions with garages beneath a sequence of airless rooms that I sometimes tried to work some pertinence into—could probably be mapped out to clarify the prevailing direction, which was toward something else.

This was a wife with sunken teeth and runny eyes and a face that darked up when she was finished talking. She had bangs—a blindfold, practically, of black hair. Nights, I watched her watch the babiness go out of her children. I think she was waiting for them to bleed together into a single, soft-boned disappointment. There were three of them, and they all had the same trouble with time—not just with telling it, but with knowing that it had passed, knowing what it separated.

Late one night when the woman had drunk herself snory, I gathered the children into the living room. The four of us sat together on the sofa, a sleepless immediate family. I decided to do justice to the children one by one. The youngest often wet his bed, so I told him: "You sweat a lot, that's all. Who doesn't?" I assured the middle child that he ate constantly not because he had a worm but because his teeth needed activity. And the oldest, whose teacher sent home notes saying that the girl had started speaking up in class about her "stepdog" and her "stepself": I had to let her egg herself on until she got a feel for the busywork of my heart. Everything came out of me in what sounded like a father's voice. I was good at stringing myself along.

The woman eventually brought her disturbances of mind to bear on getting herself under some auspices—some high-up, steep-eaved auspices for a change. There was a man made of money who owned more than one automobile, and she found a way to take charge of the one he liked the least. It was radish-colored and underslung. One night, she took me for a ride in it and explained that the man had put her to work in a vast hall, someplace altitudinous, auditoriumish, where desks were arranged on risers as far as the eye could see. She was careful to keep the man himself out of the description.

I remember looking out the passenger-side window at the mirror and the lopsided traffic it was cupping out for me to take notice of. Decaled in ghost-white letters across the face of the mirror was the claim "OBJECTS IN MIRROR ARE CLOSER THAN THEY APPEAR." This I crowdedly assented to.

Then I did a dumb thing. I moved into an apartment house and grew concerned that the person living in the unit above mine was following me, upstairs, from room to room. For much of the day, my life would be down to just this one concern. I would walk from the living room to the bedroom, or from the kitchen to the bathroom—I had just those four rooms, in that order—and there this person would be, right spang overhead, the footfalls clumpy but companionate, solicitous.

Sooner or later it dawned on me that this person had divined how things were laid out in my rooms, had rearranged the furniture and belongings and outsweepings upstairs to correspond to my own—so that if, during a passage from room to room, I abruptly stopped (lowered myself to a region of the floor where a tossed magazine had landed in a rumply heap, for instance, and then lingered over it rehabilitatively, smoothing out its pages, restoring as much as I could of its flat, unread, newsstand inviolability), there would be, at that very same spot twelve feet or so above me, a parallel distraction for this person, a consuming project of his or her own.

In other words, there was my life, my offgoings from room to room, and there was the clomping reiteration of it being carried out upstairs. So this is how I got married vis-à-vis my finishing wife: I moved myself and the person upstairs out of our apartments and into a house in another city. This wife was young enough to give birth. The birth was quick and thoughtless.

The child went through life with expressions on its face that were not its own. Bus drivers and crossing guards and food handlers demanded to know whose they were. The best I could do was see everybody's point, then look away. There was always something waiting to be looked at, someone missing out.

As for the child, unresolved questions of attribution drove it far enough out of sight for me to hold down a job. There is almost too much truth in the words when I say that I was holding the job down. The fact is that I was a weight on it, keeping it from getting done. There was a heavy, flattening incorrectness that eventually found its way to the attention of somebody not too high up.

Then came nights when, lying awake beside my final wife, I would spend too much time putting my finger on what was wrong. I was wearing the finger out.

What was wrong was very simple.

Sometimes her life and mine fell on the same day.

When You Got Back

When I wrote this originally, it was a piece on walking as a disorder of the body: walking as affliction, not function. I am relieved that no one will ever get to see it. The piece was immodest and threatening in tone. I wrote it after reading something somebody else had written, something much better and more mildly put, on an entirely different subject. I wrote it in a single sitting at a card table, an upholstered one with brown vinyl stretched rather slackly over a half-inch or so of foam rubber. That was not the best surface in the world to be writing on—there was nothing solid beneath my sheet of paper as I drove the pencil across it—but I wrote in gusts, furies, of words.

When I finished, I moved in with a woman who had been after me for months. I brought the card table, my clothes, some chairs, all the health and beauty aids I owned. I lived with the woman for a little over a year. It was difficult. She was one of the unhappily happy. We were both in love with the same man. Once a week we took a bus to his building and listened to his records. The man had plenty of pull, so the woman and I would dance together and baby each other in front of him while he resleeved some of the records in his collection, which was immense and off-limits to us. We never did have any turn of events with the man, either marriedly or privately, though I am probably just guessing on the woman's part.

When the woman's parents died—the father first, the mother some months later—I had to tag along to the viewings and the funerals. At a gathering after the second funeral, one of the relations, who was drunk, went around introducing me as the woman's "expected," which almost everybody corrected to mean "intended." Afterward, the woman drove me to the house where her parents had lived. It was a small row house in a run-down neighborhood. She took me to the room that had once been her bedroom. It was right inside the front door. It was the room that in any other household would have been the living room. A couple of days later, she moved into it.

For once, I got a real job. I was selling high-tech surveillance equipment to bosses who were losing sleep over what their employees might be up to. I was living, off and on, in an efficiency apartment with a high-school girl—a senior, I'm pretty sure. I must have been serious about the girl, because I brought some things home from the store for her, things she could easily put to work on her teachers at school.

One night, the girl was sitting at my card table and studying for a test. She wanted to read a couple of chapters and then have me ask her all the review questions at the back. She figured it would take at least two hours to do the reading. I asked her what the subject was. "Some kind of geography," she said. Without even having to be told, I took a walk. I did not even bother looking up at the window of the apartment to see if the girl was in it, with or without my phone pressed against her ear. Part of the truth I had had to keep from her was that when I was in school I had been too dumb to learn the things the teachers were teaching. I had to content myself with learning something else, other things, instead. One of them was how, when taking a walk, you had to calculate what the walk was getting taken away from—what was getting subtracted from what. You had to determine what would be left when you got back.

In the parking lot, I met a man carrying a basketful of laundry. He explained that he had just washed his clothes but there was something unutterably troubling and unfinished about what had happened. His laundry was not done, he said; it was in error. He set the basket down and tugged a pair of washed-looking pants from the tangle and shook them out in my direction.

"Vouch for me," he said.

POSITIONS

The trouble with coming was that I actually did arrive somewhere. I arrived at the place my body had already left. I got there just in time to get a good look at what had happened where things were. I looked at the person on whom I had been a passenger—in every case, my sister. I looked at this woman, who was a form of transportation, a mode of shipment.

Then what?

I think I stopped looking.

For months it was like that in exactly one room. It was a room in which everything was first on the one hand and then on the other hand, and before long the hands went back into the pockets and were out of view.

Is it coming through that I got myself entailed in her, got conveyed by her body to the room where everything had to be taken out right away but could never be put back in the exact same place because there was nothing reliable to go by?

By rights, certain things were up to me. It was up to me to make sure there was a roof over where her body came apart, where it showed what was inside, where the harsh pink activity of herself kept carrying on. We were on the second of three floors. I was the one hope.

I worked as a substitute teacher, revising a test that everybody, regardless of ability, would flunk. I had the tests printed at my own expense and had a black felt slipcase especially sewn. This is where the money went.

Every so often when I was devising a new test, my sister would notice me from the bed in a way that made me feel myself seen. Usually what she said was: "Your chair is pointed wrong." She would get up and bulk herself against the chair—I would not budge; in fact, I would solidify myself on the cushion with downward, side-to-side thrusts of my rear end—until she managed to angle things differently, influentially. Then I would have to board my sister and get delivered to where things now stood.

One day the school district was through with me. I got a letter with a many-signatured petition attached. My sister was offered a position requiring her to make sandwiches on a large scale in a building where there would be lots of steps for her to climb. On the bed were a bus schedule and an umbrella. She washed her hair in the basin. She sang to herself as she rinsed. She made me a practice sandwich, something thick and colory. She wrapped it in one of my handkerchiefs, then sat down on the bed to watch me unwrap the sandwich and eat.

I could see that the furniture had already been turned, reset, hours ahead or hours behind—whatever it took.

Her mouth did not move with mine.

Their Sizes Run Differently

There were different ways we did not come into our own.

We were warm-armed, hot-handed girls. Our palms burned. We made fists around ice cubes, or squeezed anything else frozen—boxes of vegetables, foiled cuts of meat. When they thawed, we exiled them to the freezer again, reached for whatever had collected a fresh crust of frost.

We knew how to write with a broken pencil-point if there was still a divot of exposed wood stuck to the side. We would fit what was left of the point back into the tip of the long casing, and then, seizing the pencil just above the scalloped border where the splintery wood met the yellow enamel, press down courageously, foolhardily, in the direction opposite the split. That was the only way things could get written out, everything that was spoken into us, the voice drabbing down the line of our bones. "Nature favors the delocalized heart," the voice mostly said.

We had the same oily skin, dripping and dark. We were warned never to let our hands land on our cheeks or our foreheads, told that our blotting fingerpads would make things only worse. By the end of the day, our faces would appear to be entirely behind water. It was just the rain coming back out of us, we were told. By morning, the pillowcases would be moist with our heatdrops.

At a given moment, one of us would always be the first to arrive at the unringing telephone, fetch the receiver from its cradle, then cup the sievelike speaker out for the others to have to hear. We were convinced that the dial tone did not sustain the same pitch from one day to the next—that it sometimes stepped itself up a clement half-note at the very least, and on occasion lowered itself into a register of pure rebuke.

Our conduct at the mirror was exemplary. We cut ourselves dead as we sponged our faces, groomed our teeth. We dismissed every unsolicited collateral movement in the glass. We kept ourselves secret. We were girls beyond recognition, beneath ourselves.

One day, we were led into a high-ceilinged room and told that everything had already been done for us, that nothing had been spared or held back, that we had been born for no reason other than for hair to have an extra place to grow in the world. A hand pointed to the wide route the hair was already starting to take down our calves. If you cut it, we were told, it will come back. It will haunt.

The curfew was lifted.

I went to where another girl was living and tried to live there too. There was little to be learned, but we arranged ourselves stationarily in the light she had prepared by uptipping only certain slats of the Venetian blinds. I could see down into the side yard, where she was sponsoring a line of gawky flowers. Every night we let sleep reinflict upon us its formulary and useless terrors. Come morning, it was usually argued that we were out of place, and a map was once again pencilly roughed out. I ran my hair over everything the girl drew.

One day, the girl removed a cake from a cardboard carton and explained that she had worked out a method of consumption by which she was not so much eating the cake as allowing the cake to incur a smaller, less rectangular version of itself—much as (or so she said) a body part, if left alone long enough, brings about, takes on, accumulates, the hand or mouth of somebody else, the arriving hand pointfully different in complexion and intent, and the mouth talking (concealedly) about something else entirely, such as how other people's handwriting always looks more legitimate, more artless, than one's own, one's own seeming (in comparison) suspectable, staged, *manufactured*, impeaching the misdirected fingers that still control the pencil, not to mention the arm and its gainless travels.

Am I again covering the subject of her hands and their aptitude for crisis, the left hand more adroit than the right one at communicating itself at long last to the only appropriate knee or saucer or coin? It was a hand endowed with a ruthful sense of what it might next be due on, of what (only moments later) it was to become the final fitting bearer of. I was the opposite—my body irrelevant, just the podium, the dais, from which a face had to speak. My body was where I was instead of everywhere else.

The girl of whom I speak washed herself pertinently in a marble tub. I had acquired a modest capital of gels and oils and salts with which I tinted the water. Some nights I handed her a little tablet of soap. I would follow the course, the career, of the soap as she swiped it across her chest. Other nights there was a pitted mash of fruit that she dwindled onto herself with a strip of cloth. The greasy water tilted when finally she stepped from the tub and I took her place. I became a full citizen of her water.

All too often, though, my life came along and I joined up with it—reconcerned myself with it to the full, enlisted in movement already under way, stood up to myself, made out how my body was lost on me anew. I went to stay with a girl in a building where the girl's mother lived with a woman the mother had known all her life. The girl wrote to me on her instep, and then she planked her leg out toward me so I could peel off the thick sock and read. All it said was: "How will you be mine?" It was presently decided that the girl and I would profit from learning. The night before the start of school, I confided to the girl that what I looked at I looked at only as a favor to what I was not looking at; that the nicest thing I could think to do for a person, the only way I could go out of my way for such a person, the highest compliment I could possibly pay such a person, was to see to it that I did not see the person at all; that sometimes I cheated and applied my eyesight to the person, but so cautiously, so sparingly, that the person was no more than bare shape, dim contour.

I could not take my eyes off the girl as I spoke.

In school, I was put a grade ahead of the girl. It was explained that the tartaned girls on either side of me, and those in front and behind, were my "neighbors." I kept my eyes on my own paper. The teacher would interrupt our silent reading and tell us to picture something—a different land, or an animal—and when it was an animal, I would see something knobby or protuberant on it that barely belonged and that made its life ungovernable and boonless and sad.

"Who can put it on the board?" the teacher would say.

I was quick with chalk because of how fast it dilapidated in my hand. I would hold the stick of it sidewise between thumb and forefinger, then powder the slate with cloudages that consumed panel after panel of the board. The teacher would follow behindhand, accomplishing arclike swipes with her eraser. The chalk I dropped back into the tray would be worn flat on one side.

I was eventually taken in by a woman whose daughter must have been one of the ones who had drowned. When it came time for as much as possible of my body to disappear behind that of a guitar, I had my choice of the woman's sleek, solid-body electric or the daughter's elderly Hawaiian, an acoustic, which lay in a case lined with wine-colored felt. The Hawaiian, the one I fell for, was tall and full of figure, with *f*-shaped sound holes out front and tiny cracks, crazings, running the length of its voluptuous back. I took the guitar warmly, adultly, into my arms but could not strike off even the simplest of chords. The trouble was my hands: I was no good at crippling the fingers of my left one the way it took to get the strings clenched against the fretboard and to get the chords compiled from the loose, wiry notes.

I fed pieces of underwear—panties, camisoles—into the sound holes to dampen the noiseful predicament I had carried out to the woman's driveway. I operated the strings of the guitar with a Q-tip instead of a pick. I finally contrived an open, cheater's tuning. I clamped out the chords with my thumb curling down over the fretboard. I was thus confined to the major chords, which became heinous, public tollings of my heart.

There were other downthrown girls along the road, with instruments they had never learned the right way to play: a chord organ, a snare drum with a clinky cymbal hanging boltedly and hazardously from above, another guitar—this one electric and overdecorated and plugged into a trebly midget amplifier. These girls heard what was becoming of the chords I platted out with my bone-hard thumb. The noise got onto the girls, saddled them. A group of them began to assemble around me on the blacktop. It was a jinkly, bickering music that we frittered and tingled from our instruments and into the last of the summer.

I sang the way I still talk.

Every song was the worst way I could think of to ask for what I did not yet know how not to want.

Yours

Usually the most I care to say in the morning is: "I have a couple of grown sons." I say it for the neighbors on both sides.

If I have a problem, it is this: there is a store where everything costs a dollar.

These are essentially my outsets and my outcomes.

All I am saying is pick any room and, chances are, there is already enough in it for something situationy to get started. In particular, there is a big difference in the quiet right before the phone finally rings. That is what I listen for the most. The phone itself I just let ring.

One thing else:

There are two types of people in this world.

Just don't ask me where they live.

SMTWTFS

One of the things I mean when I say I could be wrong is that it was my mother, most likely, who told me to shit or get off the pot. This would have been at the dinner table. I was probably withdrawing chips of cereal from the box and eating them one by one with my fingers.

My family: here they come for the last time if I can help it. Mother, father, sister—all of them big-boned, robustly depressed, full of soft spots and unavailing clarities when it came to me.

It was for their privacy that I took a job passing out perfume samples on the main floor at Brach's. It was a woman's fragrance. I splurged it onto my forearms and pressed the sample cards, matchbook-sized with a tiny capsule slotted inside, on men and women alike. I would watch them descend the slope of the escalator. When they stepped within the radius of my arms, the doubts would start: hadn't I already urged a sample on this person or that one? Everybody started looking recognizably unfamiliar. Now and then the supervisor would surprise me from behind and pat some more posture onto my shoulders or float a hand in the gutter of my lower spine.

When the summer was through, I set out for the cinder-block acropolis of the state-university system. My roommate's cousin lived a couple of floors down from us in the dorm and had his own refrigerator. He came from the coal region and called pens "ink pens." By the end of the first week, I had made up my mind to spend money on him. In the gloom of a movie house, I slid my hand onto his and forked our fingers together. At the sink in the restroom afterward, I gave him the conclusive kiss. I kept expecting to get smacked silly. In bed, everything was up to me and happened in the order I wanted it.

We read my roommate's tight, possessive diary every afternoon without ever once finding ourselves anywhere in the wrap-ups. One day, we slipped out of our housing contracts, took an efficiency apartment off campus. We started disinvolving ourselves from our classes more flashily. Once or twice a week we rode a bus to the closest city, a low-rise hub with a couple of perishing business streets. We ate at a department-store coffee shop, strode up and down escalators, tried things on each other in fitting rooms. Sometimes I could get him to piss delicately onto the more expensive clothes. I liked the *shreesh* that abruptly parted hangers made when I returned everything to the racks.

There were nights I could not keep him away from overdue homework—accounting, mostly: ledger sheets, a plug-in calculator with squarish raspberry digits, knife-sharpened pencils. On the floor, with an open textbook of my own ramped up onto my knees, I'd slick flesh-colored polish onto my fingernails and study a chapter—the look, the shape, of it: the sometimes stepwise progression down the page that chocks of white space made wherever paragraphs came to a halt.

One afternoon, in the Old Main concourse, I saw him sitting on one of the long, itchy sofas. There was a girl beside him, a tall leg-crosser with a haphazardry of oranged hair. They had notebooks open on their laps and were contentedly, curricularly, sifting through stacks of index cards. I started going to the city on my own. In a bar, a businessman chuffed commandingly to my side, led me to a table, bought me a big late lunch. He drove me to an office trailer at a construction site, unlocked the door.

It was through this man that I soon fell in with some damselly boys, maidens, a few years older than I. There were too many of us for the one bed, so some of us slept on the floor, on throw rugs, or with the rugs as blankets. We flavored our bathwater with things from the kitchen—fruit syrups, sometimes just soda. The one whose apartment it was, my host, got a summons for jury duty in a special mailer he had to tear open by grasping the thing at both ends and then pulling, the way you do with certain disappointing party explosives. We took turns going over the letter he wrote to get out of going. That day, he looked baffled for his age, indifferently shaved. He had gone after his hair with a blue plastic kiddie scissors, mincing it up in employment-defying ways. He was the most befucked of us, the first to start filling out. I was the one who finally mailed the letter.

He made us all go to his parents' anniversary party. His older brother was there, under a tarp, with his leg in a cast, and I was expected to write something on it. A pen, a porous-point marker, was volunteered into my hand. I had no problem getting down on the patio floor. The front part of the cast was so oversubscribed, there were regions along the slight curve above the knee that were already palimpsestic. I read from the bottom up. None of the names were ones I could put faces to. There were lots of looping longhand endorsements from women who had old names with fresh spellings: Lynnda is one I remember.

I looked at the line of downcurved toes in their cut-out wiggle room. There was a tuft of black hairs on each of the toe-knuckles. The nails were dull ovals.

"Bashful?" the brother's brother—my protector—said.

I finally signed "SMTWTFS," like on the calendar, which is what I usually did when a name got called for on a petition or guest register. The general principle, I guess, was that days were yet to come, big fat days flying in your face.

The one girl I danced with turned out to be the sister. She had swimmy eyes and flat hair and a raisinlike mole on her left cheek. Her arms were long, thin, string-colored. She kept wheeling the conversation around to her parents and brothers. "You picked the wrong one of us to rub off on you," she said.

In her room, upstairs, she had to finish most of my sentences for me. She said it was obvious I had not had my heart bounced around nearly enough. There was a pitcher of colored liquid on her nightstand, and I watched her tilt out cupful after cupful. She drank tediously, dragging it out.

When the time came, she was good at taking the light away from everything it was intended to get thrown on.

The only one who could give me a lift into town afterward was a friend of the family's I had not been introduced to. He was just barely in the age range, but he had the physique. I agreed with everything he said—that too much happens when people do not get shot and killed, that there were bound to be more at home like me, that things happening over and above did not necessarily ever make it down to the street, and that it was a wonder more people didn't do what he did, which was to recite the dinner order into the drive-through microphone, drive around the building to the pickup window, hand over the exact amount, reach for the bag, then park the car, carry the food into the restaurant, and eat at a booth, where you had secrecy.

"That way, nobody sees you asking for it," he said.

We were stuck behind a truck with a sign on the back that read: "THIS VEHICLE STOPS OFTEN."

"Turn here?" he said, motioning toward the windshield.

My hand was already on his upper arm. It was one more thing in the world my hand could fit around without ever once actually having to hold.

Being Good in October

The wedding was curt and almost entirely without result. At no point during the ceremony did the minister let anybody but himself be the center of attention. The one halfway-decent thing about the reception was that the tables were so narrow, the guests could sit on only one side. They faced the backs of the guests at the next table and kept their voices down.

When the woman got home afterward, she put everything away in drawers and cupboards so that she could not go after any of it in her sleep without waking herself up first and having to know what it was she had on her hands.

The Smell of How the World
Had Ground Itself onto
Somebody Else

From what I gather, I had to have had the sense, sooner or later, to get up and have a look at the outline my body had pressed into the carpet during sleep—the clearing I had made by pushing aside clothes and food wrappers and newspapers and such—and it could not have resembled the shape of any of the familiar postures of convalescence, because I remember thinking there were still some people, two or three people—I kept adding them together differently—who could be counted on, if reached at the right time of the month, to say, "I was just thinking about you," and these were not the people I thought to call.

The phone was one more constant thing on the floor—an old rotary-dial model with a dumbbell handset. I must have called the woman and hung on every word of mine, taken in everything I was saying, because I put clothes on and drove to the address I had repeated aloud when it was the first thing spelled out for me to write down.

She was living with a cousin and his blind dogs and porcelain dolls in a rented row house. The cousin could have been out—either at the resort where he worked or at the school he had to go to. I probably asked about everybody else, just to make sure there was conversation, or just to be pulling for somebody, or why would I now swear that the three youngest (girl, girl, girl) were with an aunt and the two oldest (girl, boy) were renting places of their own? What other reason would I have to bring any of them up? Wasn't I the one they claimed had told them things about the human body that could not possibly be true—that it was the grave the heart was buried in, and other misrepresentations of far worse ilk?

A doctor who liked the woman had written out a whole pad's worth of prescriptions, dated at two-month intervals, for a cone-shaped junior tranquilizer, and as a believer in keeping something on my stomach, I am certain I must have taken what was offered and chewed it. And then the woman had to have said, "Come under the covers," because I had only ever gone by what was visible, the parts of things that stuck right out, and what I was seeing was familiar—everything on her that gaped.

The children knew where to find the woman when it seemed reasonable to move back in. It took a couple of days. The house—this was a differently addressed one, with shutters—had three floors. Every room was going to have the same kind of blinds. Everybody who was old enough to work was going to be told how long, in weeks, she had in order to find a job. Names and deadlines were going to get written on a kitchen wall that was going to get painted harvest gold. The woman was making good money and did not have to report to anybody except her boss, who liked her and said, "No

50

need to come in today—just stay by that bonny phone of yours just in case."

At the time of which I write, my middle forties, people were expected to provide their own transportation. The car I owned was not presentable. It did not make an impression. One morning, I drove to a used-car dealership and stood at the edge of the lot. Within an hour, the salesman had me cleaning out my trunk and my back seat. It had to be done with great haste, he said. A woman was already interested in the car, he said. He wheeled over two large garbage barrels, then dragged out some cardboard boxes to hold whatever I was going to keep. He said he understood what it must be like to live in such a small place and have nowhere to go with your things.

It was the woman and the oldest girl who afterward pretended to be attorneys and made the lawyerly threats over the phone to the salesman, the sales manager, the president of the lot. None of it did any good—once you sign a contract, etc. The new car was a grating brick-red insignificancy in the woman's graveled driveway. I could look out and see the youngest three peering into the windows of it, pointing at the boxes that were too big for the trunk. The boxes did not yet belong in the house.

The oldest girl kept saying, "I won't bite you." I listened from the other end of the living room when it was her turn to talk legal into the phone. To prolong her threats, she kept up a kind of vowelly crooning between words. It was the first I had ever taken much notice of her. She appeared to be in her twenties and had arranged the freckly lengthiness of her body into a slouch that made her elbows and legs seem pointed privately, inquiringly, toward me. I started siding with her, beholding whatever she beheld—the fishbowl ashtray, the dishful of pastilles and drops, the plum-colored splotch she kept rubbing on her shin.

As thanks, I said I would take the two of them, the woman and the oldest girl, out to dinner, someplace decent and scarcely lit. The girl went upstairs and took a long, decisive shower—I could hear all the water it was taking—and then came down in a slip and kneeled in front of the coffee table and looked up into my face as she applied the determining makeup.

At the restaurant, she asked me questions about herself—what I thought she thought, which violences I considered her capable of—and no matter what I said, she would say, "That's a good answer," or "How right you always are."

"But you're so far away," she said, finally.

We were seated at a banquette, the girl in the middle. The woman kept getting up to call her boss.

For maybe two or three nights afterward, I fell asleep on my floor by starting with the woman under my eyes, then adding on the two-inch advantage every new generation supposedly gained over its predecessor, lightening and lengthening the hair, overpowdering the face, inflating the biceps, spattering freckles onto the arms and chest, until I had brought the girl on top of me in her avid, breastless entirety.

As always, I was slow to let on that I knew how far I was being taken advantage of. The girl fell in with some friends of her cousin's, tight-lipped teenagers in floppy shorts that came down to their shins. That was the last I saw of her for years.

One night, I stupidly told the woman how I felt.

"That's all going to change," she said.

Instead, the woman opted for misery and hardship and unemployment of a high order. These were the years of learning disabilities, loosenesses of mind, downheavals all over. I went through her thick mail. I remember disconnection notices, policy cancellations, bounced-check statements, form letters declaring who was suspended from school and for how long, collection-letter sequences whose initial entry always started with the question "Have you forgotten something?"

What I kept forgetting was that I was nothing to anybody under that roof other than the one who stuck around for it to repeatedly dawn on everybody else—her relations, mostly; the cousin above all—that it takes all kinds. In time, the oldest girl came back. She arrived in a car of her own. Most of her hair was gone. This was the smallest house yet, a cottage. It was still daylight out on the porch. I could see that the girl was looking into the uncurtained window, already figuring herself back onto the furniture.

"You were going to say something," she said in my direction. "You were going to put something to me," she said.

"A proposition," she said.

The woman had to step outside in her graphic housecoat and explain to the girl that there was nowhere for the girl to sleep.

I could describe the circles the other children left the house to move around within. I could describe the walks of life to which they applied themselves. I could describe the beds they slept astray. I would not be the first. There is already a beaten path.

The least I can say is that once in who knows how long you actually get to see where you are living. I can attest to this plentifully. I can speak from experience something awful. Just this once, you have your chance: all the right lights are finally on.

Your first thought is to let somebody else take over the talking.

That summer, the two of us rolled what was left of my pennies—there were still basinsful of them, drawersful that went all the way back to my youth—and I drove the woman to where there was one large body of water, and then on to where there was another, and then on yet again. There were always seagulls, a span of boardwalk, waves, shells to accumulate in our drinking cups. But it was never the sea, she claimed. Show me a sea, she said.

I was a thoroughgoer. There was so much to go back on.

Years must have gone by without my fingering getting any better. The woman kept saying: "A little lower."

Or: "Not even close."

Or: "Do you even know where you are?"

It says something about my wife, which is what the woman had become, that I am saying any of this so voluminously. Because if you are anything like me— *please be*—you have had the sense to keep yourself under investigation long enough to already know what is in store.

For instance, walking in on her when she is transferring everything from one handbag to the other.

Does she say: "Finish your meal"?

Or: "All you do is make work"?

Or: "Occupy yourself"?

In my case, there were only a couple of spots left for me to still fill. One was at work. This was the spot in which I had found out I was not being paid the same as everybody else. I was in the washroom, soaping my hands at the sink, when I heard my name come up in conversation in the stalls behind me. Whomever the voices belonged to had got hold of a printout of how much everybody was making. A distribution. I rinsed my hands and dried them on a paper towel and got out of there in one two three.

Later in life, I brought the matter up with a supervisor. I got called a malcontent, a troublemaker, more hindrance than help. What could she do but put me behind a desk even farther from the public? She took me off light-administrative and put me on time sheets. Work was brought to me in carts.

"Do your dirt on numbers for a change" is all the other one—the one who always gave straight answers—told me to my face.

One other spot I was in—the last—was the one at whose center I kept getting even worse at judging the distances between people. I fouled up every time. If I saw somebody declaring herself with a gesture, I intercepted as much as I could of whatever was on its way to whom it might have actually concerned. I helped myself to anything headed elsewhere. I carried on as if it were mine.

Do I have to draw a picture? The one I keep drawing and shoving in her face is the one of me walking home from work one day when she had the car. I passed a store where a kid was sitting along a landscaped strip that bordered the parking lot. The kid had its arms wrapped around its shins, knees pointing up.

"I cut myself," the kid said to me.

I stopped for a look. I saw a knee with a scab that looked picked-at. A few platelets of scab were loose and afloat in what little blood there was.

The scab was the color of ham. Burnt ham.

I took the clean handkerchief out of my back pocket, squatted next to the kid, patted the handkerchief against the knee. A few circlets of blood appeared on the face of the cloth.

I said something along the lines of: "Just keep that on there for a while."

And here comes what your life will never be the same after which, the same way mine has already never been: my face was bent right over the kid's other knee. The knee was aimed right at me.

I got a whiff of it, all right. I got the hell out of there.

Who hasn't lived life expressly to avoid having to one day inhale something that entire? It was the complete, usurping smell of how the world had ground itself onto somebody else.

Did I hasten home and shut myself in the bathroom and try to bring forth a similar smell—something equally total—from my own knees? Did I wait until my wife had fallen asleep and then expect to drag its like out of hers? Did I slip out of bed and put my clothes back on, let myself out of the house, steer a straight course toward the parking lot at the store, roll up the legs of my pants, grind my kneecaps into the damp earth until the dirt was caked onto the flesh, then roll the pants down again, plunge home, sneak into the bathroom, disrobe, remount the toilet, bury my nose in my knee, and draw in big, hopeful breath-gulps to satisfy myself that the disrupting magnificence on the kid's knee—the alarm—had been nothing more than the neglected pressing smellsomeness of dirt alone; and having discovered, instanter, that it was not a matter of dirt, that the point of origin—of contact—lay elsewhere, did I spend the next couple of weeks before and after supper wending my way around the purlieus of the store, the alleys and backyards and traffic islands, keeping my gait brisk and neighborish, doing my best to preserve the appearance of an unprovoked, unprowling fellow in walking shorts first working up an appetite, then strolling off his meal, but always ultimately, futilely, rubbing the knees against something differently frictional—tree bark or smoothed rock, the blacktop of a driveway or nettles in a vacant lot?

Did I ever once in all of this time bring off anything remotely approximating a get-together with my wife? Did it eventually occur to me to seek out the kid itself? Did I have any luck? Did I have enough sense to burst into my supervisor's office and make a clean breast of it? Did I say: "This is what I've done. This is what I'm doing. This is what I will have done by the time I'm finished"? Because if people should happen to ask, it will be only because they themselves are already sick of being pestered for the answer. The identical let-down looks on their faces are the only way the hostess can tell for sure that the people are all in the same party the one time it occurs to them to venture out to eat as a community.

So go ahead.

Make anything up.

Tell them whatever their little hearts desire.

Tell them I was an only son at the time the world was filling up with women, making everything harder for me to see.

SUSCEPTIBILITY

This is about two people. It should not have to matter which two. In fact, wherever there are two people, regardless of what everything between them might still be in spite of, this is bound to be the story in full.

One of them wanted to know where he could buy some of those rubber squares you stick under the feet of furniture, either to protect the finish on the floor or to keep the furniture from sliding away, whichever it was.

That one's my father.

The other one's me.

Rims

From the look of things, there were some openings left in the band, some spaces not yet filled, so I got called out of study hall one afternoon and led into a storage room, where I was told to pick an instrument. I pointed to the first thing I saw that I could play with my mouth shut: a drum. I let them thread sticks through my fingers and strap the snare drum onto me. I let them lead me into the band room and up to the top tier, where the other drummers were already standing. I let them show me which ones to stand between.

I dribbled out a long, mushy roll that was not what I meant. Then I tried a slow, tappy single-stroke roll that did not come any closer. I did some paradiddles. I splatted out some flams and some rim shots.

The band performed popular songs that were brassed up and flattened out to sound like marches. I kept my mouth closed and my lips still while I played everything wrong by heart. Then I taught myself something better. I brought the sticks down to within a fraction of an inch of the drum's head and just pattered away at the air. I got away with this on football fields, in parades.

There were eight other drummers in the band: five on snares, two on bass, one on cymbals. I received them one by one in the closet where the drums were stored. It never took me very long to get the boys to where I could feel the air go out of them. I got to them first. The girls got what was left. I was doing everybody a favor—slowing the boys down for the girls, making the boys easier for the girls to take. I got between the boys and the girls and clouded up their hearts.

Nights, there was family history for me to go down into, but only so far. I lived with my grandmother above a garage. I made all the meals and changed all the subjects. On garbage night, my grandmother sent me to the curb in one of my mother's things—almost always the brown floral-print dress, the sleeveless one, that she wore in the snapshots. I kept throwing it away, balling it at the bottom of a wastebasket, and it kept getting retrieved and laid out for me to wear. My grandmother watched from a high window as I set the bags down along the curb. I think she found passing references to my mother in the slope of my arms and the blond disorder of my hair. Afterward, in my underwear, I would sleep in the position that put me farthest from everywhere I came from.

One day, the band director finally said, "Why don't you quit the band if you think it's beneath you to play?"

We were in his office, with the door shut. Somebody knocked.

"Hold your horses," the band director shouted at the door.

I looked from his face to the smudgy nameplate on his desk and to the door, which had a poster on it from a musical-instrument supply house. I was looking from thing to thing. You can look at a thing until it gets looked away with once and for all. You can take the thing and just look at it until it gets all looked out. Then you can go on to the next thing and start over. You can keep doing this with whatever gets lined up in front of you to have to see.

This is one way you can go through the whole world.

Esprit de l'Elevator

There were three of them left—sometimes four. Parked not in the lobby but in the gallery above the lobby, though that makes the place—the building, the apartment house—sound classier than it was.

Maybe an overhang is all it was called. An overlook. Mezzanine?

It was set up like a living room—stuffed chairs, a coffee table, a bookcase with a few magazines. There was a railing so people would not have to spill over into the lobby proper.

These three watched me walking out of and back into the building a varying number of times per day. I was working on bringing the number down to maybe three or four.

I was getting nowhere.

The only progress I was making was remembering to carry something on my way out—a big envelope or a sealed box that looked ready to be taken to the post office. The envelopes and boxes piled up in the back of my car. Some night, I kept telling myself, I was going to stay up late and carry everything back up and start using it all over again.

A part of me said, "Why bother to go get it when it might come to me in my sleep?" I was almost always in the trough of a nap, my arms over the sides, digging around in the carpet.

I kept washing my hands of what the hands kept doing regardless.

Balcony.

Three of the times were for breakfast, lunch, supper.

The rest were for what I was still hungry for.

I carried things up from my car in small plastic bags.

I had different things I did to wear each day thin.

The three were two retired women, or widows, and one fat young security guard, male. The occasional fourth was the oldest retarded person I had ever seen. She had to be pushing sixty. I had never been close enough to make out if the glasses were bifocals. Sometimes when there was no way for me to get around walking past, I nodded hello and she would give me a wide berth. Other times she waved a finger.

I was the only one who trusted the elevator.

Not a security guard for the *building*. He security-guarded someplace else.

One afternoon, I was in the laundry room—I had all three machines going—when he pudged in to throw some trash down the chute. What I was wearing had already been worn.

"Washday?" he said, loud enough for the other two on the balcony to hear.

As always, I had no answers, nothing to put a stop to their wonderings. That night, I began to set down the full account of my tenancy. It became a book of earnest libels. I had three copies copied—one for each. Herewith excerpts:

How often do you get it?

Spend enough time with a person—coincide in the same room, achieve a reasonable congruence—and you will get a feel for, a glimpse of, the party you are sitting in for. It was like this with each of the women. A party sooner or later began to assume a shape in the space between us. I took an interest. I eventually began to court this party more diligently than each of the women could bother to herself. One day this party took me by storm.

Who foots the bills?

I signed up to teach a night class at the high school, an extension course, no credit, for people who had forgotten how to sleep. It took me a weekend to throw the materials together. I baked up a big fat loaf of case histories, pattern practices, whatever else came to mind, then had copies run off. The first night, I wrote on the chalkboard the reasons people got bilked out of sleep. Afterward, I showed the students a trick, a mnemonic stunt, they could use to remember everything I had just said. They were mostly vast lactic women and self-heckling men in coats buttoned all the way up. All of them stayed after class to show me what they had taught themselves—the feats and magics, the shortcuts and so forth. A man ran me through his eye-sealing exercises, his fingers guiding mine. "I'm not up on myself and what I might still do," he told me. Sometime after dawn we went our separate ways.

What's inside the bags?

Some days my trouble is nothing more than the heavy concentration of both parents in my body. E.g., my father's tendency, at mealtide, to add extra steps to everything he did—cf. my habit of reaching for my tumbler with my left hand and passing it along to the right hand before I take my first sip. In my father's case, the route things took from hand to mouth got longer and longer. Hence for years I have been amassing ingredients for a meal I am no longer in any position to cook.

And your mother?
I am a disgruntled mourner.

Brothers or sisters?
People coming out of the cathedral and crossing the street to their cars expected traffic to part compliantly for them—they held up their hands in hopeful, crossing-guard gestures—and my sister was the only one who kept right on going, not even slowing down. She had some empty boxes in the back seat that I was going to get to use as tables—lampstands, nightstands, washstands, however I saw fit.

Reason for leaving last full-time position?
One morning, the supervisor stuck his head into my doorway and, taking in the undeserved spaciousness of the office, asked whether I thought I could maintain my level of performance if an additional employee were assigned to the room. Having always been sympathetic toward whoever has hired me when he discovers, by galling degrees, the set of fixations I bring to bear on even the most perfunctory of tasks, I said yes. A second desk was presently steered into the office. A man was brought in to sit at the desk with his back toward me. By the end of the first hour, my every movement had

become an exact but involuntary belittlement of his swivelings, his head-tossings and hair-sweeps, the flights of his arms. I felt thrown off my body. The accuracy went out of my work.

Why can't you stay put?
I have always gone to great lengths to keep my life away from the places where I have lived. People driven from themselves are always the ones you see the most of. They make themselves aggressively public. You find them in parks and municipal buildings. They see to it that as much as possible gets rubbed off, ground away, on the chairs and benches in lobbies and waiting rooms, on the tooth-yellow porcelain of courthouse toilets. They make any store or auditorium look fuller than it actually is. They eat at take-out places, the ones with just a couple of tables. "For here or to go?" they get asked, as if there were a choice.

Describe your best marriage to date.
My affiliation with—but never entirely a marriage to—a woman who worked briefly at the high school grew out of a series of conversations a man and I had about his son. The man would talk for hours about the son—how people swore by the haircuts he gave, even though he was not licensed or even certificated as a stylist, had in fact had no formal training, cut only when and where he felt like it, whenever the mood came over him; and as the man talked, the woman—whom I had known only by the rosacea in her cheeks, concolorous with my own—would gain some ground, make headway. I left the man's house one night and cornered her at the library. She had a magazine open in front of her. Her shoes were already off.

I remember that every morning, for the first couple of weeks, we took a kind of roll of everything we owned—called out the names of the appliances, the fixtures, the articles of clothing. Each day, there would be fewer things of hers to include in the tally. Before long, to save time, shirts, blouses, pullovers, sweaters, etc., became simply "tops." (This was her idea.) In like manner, other things became just broad categories of things. We lived in an "area," I was her "associate." She brought me around to her way of passing the time: doing away with the individual filth of minutes—she would move about the room and point superiorly, reprovingly, at scratchy increments of my beard, oily glosses on the slope of her nose—and gutting the hour down to the slow-turning spine of the day. (The clock itself was a square-faced wall unit with a slipping, partisan second hand that was easily derided.) She arrived, in sum, at the age she thought suited her and then halted there.

For the longest while, everything got carried over into the way she filled in for people at work—the vacationers and no-shows, people needed in other buildings. She took their places with conviction. She installed herself behind their partitions. She uncramped her legs in the wells beneath their workstations. She helped herself to the little budgets of condiments, of salt, in their drawers. She drank long, telling draughts from their mugs. The bottoms of her forearms stuck persuasively to the armrests of their chairs.

Then people, employees, were suddenly no longer going anywhere. They no longer missed work or needed to be spelled. They resettled themselves in their chairs, restocked their drawers, reared their stack trays still higher. The day she had to be let go, she went to the administrators and pleaded, then came home to abridge things even further.

What would be visible to a knocker at your door if you opened the door six inches, then a foot, then a foot and a half? That is, from a knocker's perspective, describe bigger and bigger slivers of vestibular floorscape, with an emphasis on what would most likely stand out.

Six inches: a selection of plastic bags, each with its original contents, arranged calendarially against the closet door.

Foot: the last of the exact words.

Foot and a half: men and women both—her and me in general.

CLAIMS

If I go so far as to say that at this point I had a friend,
the most it can possibly mean is that once a year,
toward the end of it, I had to drive from wherever I
was letting myself be lived, wherever I had given
consent for my life to keep being done to me, and this
friend-person had to drive from his own whereabouts,
just so we could meet for lunch in a sandwich shop
where, years earlier, while schooling together, we had
flirted with each other impatiently, wrongheartedly. By
then, things were always his idea. He was the one who
kept talking as if there would always be room in the
world for whatever he might say. I was merely the one
who kept clearing space. The thing I was good at was
keeping things sufficiently placeless for whoever's turn
came next.

Every year, he told me the same story—he had a
double life and was going to have to do something big
and final about it pretty soon. He explained that by day
he sat at his engineering desk and threw together
bridges and such for governments, and that by night he
bogged himself down in department-store men's
rooms, adult bookstores, highway rest stops. Year after
year, I listened to him tell me this.

So I said to this friend-person, "Apart from that, other than the as-per-usuals, what are we harping on?"

He repeated everything already said. There was no other matter for the facts to get wrapped around. In his voice was the enormous gloating noise of somebody standing up for his rights.

I made the mistake of looking at our waitress, who was setting plates down in front of us. It was a mistake because sometimes when you look at someone, especially someone young, you get too good a look. You see the life heaved messily, meagerly, into the person. You get a sense of the slow-traveling trains of thought, the mean streaks and off-chances, everything that has had to be crossed out or memorized so far. The parts out front—the eyes; the teeth and tongue inside the open, moving mouth—look cheap and detachable, unset, just barely staying put.

What I am saying is that through all this, all through this, I was only loosely in the midst of myself, already lapsing my way into whoever this waitress was, organizing myself within the dark of the body she was sticking up for herself inside.

THE BRIDE

If this is to be a story instead of what it was initially intended to be—an answer to the question of how you go about finding an outlet for what you are not sure is in there to begin with—then there might as well be two women instead of just one and, for a change, just the one man, who is no longer the one I threw my body away on but just somebody where I work, somebody with little say over what it is I do, which, I gather, is to look lonely from afar.

Which leaves how many more for me to pretend not to see? Because I have actually had people—persons—call me up and plead with me not to think about them. Persons who actually called me up and said: "Promise me."

I am leaving out my brother because of what he said—or what was reported to me that he had said—when there was every chance that I would not be coming to his wedding, which was to be held many hundreds of miles from where I was going to try to be asleep. What he is said to have said was: "If he don't come to mine, I don't go to his." It was probably that alone—the veiled compliment in it—that got me on the bus.

I did not kiss this bride on the church steps. This bride called me "catty" to my face not long afterward, but now that there are children, she tells me her troubles the first chance she gets.

Mine—my trouble—is that if you got a good look at my wrists—if they were all you had to see of the world—you would swear you were looking at a twenty-year-old girl and not at a man pushing past forty.

So I understandably keep my sleeves rolled up and try to downplay the rest of me and keep it farther from the masses.

I am waiting to be addressed as Miss? Miss?

It is this alone they must mean when they keep pleading there is no such thing as a stupid question.

EDUCATION

Not long after my youth blew over, I was offered a stipend to help speed along the development of a girl who was being raised in one of the old walled towns in the northern part of the state. I signed the papers and gave away my things. The next morning, I said good-bye to some people I thought might recognize me from the corridors of the building where I had been living. A couple of the older ones unlimbered their arms in a way that I regarded as a wave.

It took me several days to reach the town on foot. The girl's mother and grandmother were waiting for me outside the gates. They were seated on a rock and eating fruit out of basins on their laps.

"She's at home," the mother said. "We were told to keep her away from the school."

"How long does it usually take?" the grandmother said.

Both of them were blunt-nosed and sleep-marked. They kept themselves busy with the fruit. They kept their eyes off me.

"Let me have a look at the girl," I said.

Every afternoon, I walked the girl to the center of town. There were eight streets that led to it, and for each approach to the two blocks of shops and vaguely public-looking buildings, I assigned the town a different name: Townville, Cityton, Burgborough, Townburgh, Boroville, Cityboro, Burghton, and Town City.

With a clear conscience I would stand with the girl in the center of town and point things out—entablatures, drinking fountains, skymarks, misspelled signs in shopwindows, a pair of roofed-over stairwells, resembling subway entrances, that led citizens down to a vast, underlit comfort station. I would ask the girl: "Where are we today? Which town is this? Can you tell?"

She was young, with rude eyes and a block of thick black hair. Her stalky legs were always splodged with bites.

She would narrow her body into the shape, the posture, of answering. "Townton," she would say.

"Not even close," I would have to tell her.

After supper, while the girl played in the yard, the mother and the grandmother would call me into the bedroom they shared.

"What are her chances?" they would say. "How is she to the touch? What should be coming next? Are you going to be doing us all a world of good? What kind of timetable are you on? What should we be looking for? What are the signs?"

The house had two floors, and in no time I had the girl calling them the Land of the Upstairs and the Land of the Downstairs.

"Making them lands—what does that do?" the mother asked me when the girl was outdoors.

The room they gave me had a cot, a table, a washstand with a basin. There was no door. I was pretty certain that there had once been one and that they had had it taken down before I came.

Every night, after the girl was in bed, the mother and the grandmother would appear in the doorway.

"How soon?" they would ask.

"Too early to tell," I would say.

In the late afternoons, after our walk into town, I would smatter the names of stars and crops and oceans into the girl. I got facts off my hands and onto hers. She built tiny empires out of the facts and let me see inside them. She was warm to the touch. "You can do this," I said, putting her hands on things. The girl's father, I gathered obituarily, had worn V-neck T-shirts. The girl's heart, I also learned, was set on the slice of florid skin in the mouth of the V. I set her heart elsewhere. I lined things up in the room and pointed at them. I made her put her hands on everything.

The girl had some books of her own, books that her mother and grandmother had not known were in the house. She brought the books to me one at a time, and I told her what was wrong with what they said. They were all about the human body, its depths and its scope. I had to refute every one of the books sentence by sentence. The errors could take days, weeks, to correct. The girl wrote down the corrections, and later, while she napped, I checked over her work, making changes where they were called for, praising her penmanship wherever it deserved praise.

Together, in the yard, without knowing what the right tools would have been, the girl and I built partitions, platforms, folding screens. I remember her turning the earth with the claw of a hammer.

I started blindfolding the girl for the walk into town. When we reached the center, I would take the blindfold off and ask: "Where must we now be?"

The girl was always wrong.

Some nights there were abrupt disorders of where the girl's heart got put. The mother and the grandmother would summon me to the girl's room.

"Do something," they would cry.

I would recite the names of the towns and list the hallmarks, the quiddities, of each town, the area first in square yards and then in square meters, the principal creeks and ditches, the annual rainfall, the population, the manufactures, the number of hospital beds per dozen inhabitants, the elevation, the significant history.

After I finished, I would run over the list again, changing all the facts.

I would watch the girl's mouth.

I would hear a voice getting ready to come.

The mother and the grandmother would not leave the room.

What the mother and the grandmother fed the girl every night, what she ate with us at the table—the cleverly sliced meats, the vivid salads, the cubed potatoes—became the foundation on which, afterward, in my room, with the mother and the grandmother gawking from the doorway, I built swaying towers of candy and pretzel sticks in the girl's stomach. "This is important," I would say. The girl stood still as I patted the food into her mouth. "The towers," I explained, "are the beginnings of a city."

Then my six months were up. My stipend had run out. One day I announced to the mother and the grandmother that I would be leaving the next morning.

"Stay," they said.

"Finish," they said.

They showed me all the leeway they had where their legs went their separate ways. A slucky sound came from their groins, as if a drain were being opened.

I slept off and on with the mother and let the grandmother do what she could to me in the mornings when there was feeling in her hands.

"I remember the day it happened to her mother," the grandmother said to me one morning. "In those days, it was called 'turning ugly.' People would say, 'Did your girl turn ugly yet?' In this case, they sent a messenger from the school. He had a piece of paper. It said, 'Come and get your girl.' She was standing on the steps of the school when I got there. She said, 'The teacher knows.'

"I took her out of that school and had her put in a different one, a smaller one. I sewed her a whole new wardrobe. I told her to make believe she was bashful. She tried her best to become friends with a girl who walked with a limp. She held doors open for the girl and wrote her cheery notes on stationery she bought with her allowance. The girl always wrote back, on plain tablet paper, 'The feeling is ridiculously not mutual.' I would find the notes—dozens of them, all saying the same thing—behind the bookcase in her room. In those days, we didn't know what we know now."

I had the girl in my room. She was sitting on my table, her legs beating open and closed, like wings.

"Tell me something," I said. "Do you have a favorite place?"

"I like them all," she said.

"Each and every?"

77

"Each but not every."

She flapped her legs.

"Let me see," I said.

She got up and disrobed.

There was nothing to see.

"Which town will you move to?" I asked the girl one night after supper.

"I'll stay here," she said.

Another night, the girl came to my room on her own.

"What else are you?" she said. "Are you anything else?"

Early one morning, I was awakened by the girl's shrieks. I hurried to her room and found the mother and the grandmother already there.

"Let her cry her face loose," the grandmother said. "Let it slide right off her head. Let her learn. She has to learn sooner or later."

The girl wept into her palms.

"She went out for a walk by herself last night, after we were all asleep," the mother said.

"Filthy little thing," the grandmother said.

"She walked all over the place, high and low," the mother said.

"She went the whole way into town."

"Which town?" I said.

The crying got worse.

That afternoon, the girl came to my room to show me that it was there, in place—bristling below the slope of her belly, an isosceles shag of curls.

IT COLLECTS IN ME

Here is a story in the worst way. I have no business being anywhere in it. It comes between me and the life I have coming.

Look: a man who is not me but whose accomplishments are similar (he was the son of some parents, got himself schooled around, circumstanced himself aplenty, placed himself squarely and irreversibly in the employ of somebody who could be counted on to walk all over him, etc.) found a new way to cheat on his wife. This was not the way that everybody else was cheating at the time.

Can I skip over what was popular then without leaving anything to the imagination? Because the imagination has to be left out of this. I would hate for something to have to get created here. That is the last thing I want.

Do me a big favor and take my word that this man I am talking about was a man who paid ridiculous attention to what his wife said and did, what she wore, what she cooked. He took a hectic, grisly interest in everything about her. In bed, he fucked her to the nth degree—never let his mind wander.

What else went on between the man and the woman should go without saying, but it won't. It can't. It keeps showing up in my mouth.

It collects in me.

As it stands, at work one day I struck something up with this man—a little something. I tried to get him at one end of a conversation that had me at the other end. Do you know what the son of a bitch said?

He said, "I'm a married man."

"Personally?" is what I said.

"Go back to work," the man said.

This took place where you're supposed to go if you have an accident, if you get something on you. In fact, it did more than take place. It took up a large area of where we were. It seized it right from around us. We got pushed through each other.

He emerged from me and vice versa, I figure.

I watched him walk off in the direction of where the work was.

This is another way of saying that once, not too long ago, I wrote things down—everything.

A couple of days later, I read with great interest what I had written.

I was a great many far cries from myself.

CERTAIN RIDDANCES

The boss had a long list of reasons for letting me go—most of which, I am ashamed to admit, were generously understated. It's true, for instance, that I hogged the photocopier for hours on end and snapped at whoever politely—deferentially—inquired about how much longer I would be. I was intent on achieving definitively sooty, penumbral effects to ensure that copies looked like copies, and that, of course, took time. Some days I spent entire afternoons reproducing blank sheets of paper, ream after ream, to use instead of the "FROM THE DESK OF—" notepads the boss kept ordering for each of us.

It's also largely true that I had never bothered to learn the names of any of my co-workers. Everybody was either Miss or Sir. I am talking about people with whom I had shared a water fountain and a single restroom for years, people whose office wardrobes I had inventoried in pocket notebooks, people whose sets of genitals had often steamed only inches from my own. Actually, I *had* known their names but could just never stoop to using them. Most days what I felt was this: the minute you put a first name and a last name together, you've got a pair of tusks coming right at you (i.e., Watch out, buddy). But on days when I didn't disapprove of everybody on principle—days when the whole cologned, cuff-shooting ruck of my co-workers didn't repulse me from the moment they disembarked from the sixth-floor elevator and began squidging their way along the carpeted track that led to the office—my thinking stabbed more along these lines: A name belittles that which is named. Give a person a name and he'll sink right into it, right into the hollows and the dips of the letters that spell out the whole insultingly reductive contraption, so that you have to pull him up and dance him out of it, take his attendance, and fuck some life into him if you expect to get any work out of him. Multiply him by twenty-two and you will have some idea of what the office was like, except that a good third of my colleagues were female.

My real problem, of course, was that I could dispatch an entire day's worth of work in just under two hours. It's not that I was smart—far from it. But I was quick. I knew where things should go. I had always liked the phrase "line of work," because to me there actually *was* a line, raying out to the gridded, customered world from my cubicle, with its frosted plastic partitions that shot up all around me but gave out a few feet shy of the tiled, sprinkler-fixtured ceiling.

With so much extra time on my hands, I had to keep myself busy with undertakings of my own. For instance, there was a young woman, a fine-boned receptionist, who each day veiled her legs with opaque hosiery of a different hue, never anything even remotely flesh-toned. Every morning when I passed her desk, I would glance at her calves to note the shade. I soon began keeping track of the colors in a special file vaulted in the upper-right drawer of my battered dreadnought of a desk. Once, on my lunch hour, I made a special trip to a drugstore near the office to soak up the entire palette of hosiery shades—off-black, coffee, smoke, stone, mushroom, misty gray—because I wanted my record to be precise. Eventually I began to worry that beneath the cloak of the receptionist's hosiery the flesh of her legs was crisply diseased. The worry enlarged and clamored itself into a conviction. Soon it became critical for her to understand the extent of what I had on her. On the first of each month, I began slipping into her mail slot a little unsigned booklet—an almanac, really—with unruled four-by-six index cards for covers. The booklet consisted of as many pages as there had been days in the previous month, and each page recorded the date, the shade of the hosiery she had worn that day, and an entirely speculative notation about the degree of opacity and what it implied about whatever man had been entrenched in her the night before (sample: "June 6, charcoal, glaucomatous— how remarkably hateful of you and your niggard"). All of this would be jittered out in a near-gothic script with a calligraphy pen bought especially for the purpose in a hobby store on an overbright Sunday afternoon. By and by, I would find each booklet tacked to the bulletin board above the Xerox machine, along with a memo from the boss saying: "This must stop."

There was another woman, a pouncy administrative assistant, with a pair of succinct, pointed breasts— *interrogative* breasts. Even though I smeared past her in the corridor, wordlessly, no more than once or twice a week, I would feel grilled, third-degreed, for hours or even days afterward. At first, whenever the pressure to respond was acute—maybe every other day—I would simply slide an anonymous, index-carded "True" or "False" into her mail slot. But my responses eventually thickened into essays—with longish, interjaculatory asides about my lactose intolerance, my disloyalties, the gist and grain of my extracubicular life—and then into sets of dampish, insinuative memoirs, some of which kept me slumped over my desk for days at a time. These, too, which I photocopied until the words got shadowed and blurry, would wind up pinpricked to the bulletin board, with pealing cautionary memos from the boss.

The last response I sent her—and the only one that didn't end up flapping at me from the corkboard—was a twenty-three-page streak of reminiscence about a belated birthday gift I had received from my grandfather a few days after I turned ten years old. What he had mailed me was a big, gleamless omnibus set of board games. On the lid of the box, the words MY TREASURE CHEST OF GAMES: A DIFFERENT GAME FOR EVERY DAY OF EVERY WEEK OF THE YEAR were spelled out in runny, unweighted block letters. Inside were an arrowed cardboard spinner, a pair of bleary, chalkish dice, an unwaxed deck of playing cards, some plastic markers, a dozen or so flimsy, tri-fold game boards, each printed on both sides, and an unstapled book of instructions. The whole set struck me as trappy and degrading. I felt as if somebody else's life were being lowered over mine and that it would remain there, bestraddling and overruling, for a whole year. I remember tearing up each of the game boards—they were easy enough to shred—and bedding the pieces of each board on a separate sheet of construction paper and then balling it all up and depositing each scrumpled ball in a different wastebasket. Our house was full of wastebaskets, more than one to a room, because of the people we were intent on becoming. When my grandfather died, about a year later, and I got coaxed into attending the viewing, I noticed a spatter of paint—*hobby* paint, I was convinced—on each lens of his bifocals. Nobody had bothered to scrape it off, or else somebody had made a big point of not scraping it off. On a lamped lectern near the entrance to the chapel was a big book open to a page that everybody at the viewing was supposed to sign with a bead-chained pen. Where my name should have gone, I remember writing: "It goes to show."

The intern I left alone. The intern was just some college kid, a carrel-bound girl with a face full of sharp, unkissed features. She was only twenty, twenty-one tops, and yet there she was, assigned as much square-footage as I occupied after nine soiling, promotionless years. I had banked a digital alarm clock atop a butte of telephone directories on my shelf, and after lunch I would watch 1:12 virus into 1:13, 1:14, 1:15, and I would wish for enough dexterity to fold a paper airplane and then deftly sail it through the space we shared above the partitions, landing it on her desk. But what would I have typed—and left starkly unphotocopied—inside? "Be glad you're not the one who's going to relieve himself on a certain something the next time the boss walks out of the restroom with his suit jacket still hooked on the back of the door"?

The boss was a large man with intricately redefined dentition—a mouthful of wirework and porcelain. His eyes were slow and halting: they arrived at what they were supposed to be looking at only after lots of embarrassed trial and error. The morning he summoned me to his office to recommend that I take the first of a series of renewable leaves of absence, I kept my eyes on the cuneiform scatter of golf tees on his glass-plated desktop. The boss inquired about my "home life" and my "social life," but he talked mostly about his own. He had a teenage son, he explained, who was taking accelerated classes in high school and also a college course in art history on Saturday mornings. He had to chauffeur the kid to the college, because the kid was afraid to drive, and then he had to kill two and a half hours walking around the campus. The textbook for the course cost ninety dollars, he said, and, stealing through its glossy pages one night while the kid was out of the house, he discovered that the kid had styled tank tops and jockstraps onto the male nudes.

"What about you?" the boss said, reaching for a form I was supposed to fill out. "Are you involved with anyone?"

"Everybody," I said.

Because my body was shacky and provisional, I kept it buried beneath flopping, oversized brown corduroy suits. I had exactly six suits—all identical, all purchased from the same discount outlet on the same day, almost ten years earlier. At first, people had predictably, pityingly, said: "He only has the one suit." But eventually their tune changed to: "The guy must have a *hundred* suits!" The once steep and erect wales had been worn down until they were almost level with the wide gutters running between them.

It was in one of those eroded suits that I found some part-time work on the night shift at an office where two dozen or so employees, mostly students and housewives, looked up account numbers on microfiche screens and then penciled the numbers onto mint-green computer sheets. The turnover was high, and I was always the only male. Every time somebody new reported for work, she would see me in my suit and plump toward my desk. I would have to wave her off in the direction of the supervisor, a tasseled, doubtful black woman.

The supervisor began her nightly announcements, a third of the way through the shift, by bleating, "Listen up, girls." I would always sense the eyes of my co-workers on me when, instead of cleaving to my work for a manful, face-saving half-minute or longer before lifting my head and swiveling in the direction of the supervisor, I would swing around secretarially at the instant the word *girls* was expelled from her mouth.

I felt privileged.

Unless the landlady counted the number of times water ran in the bathtub, there was no way for her to know that I was no longer living alone. By his own choice, the kid never left the apartment, and we never fought, so what else was there for her to hear? I dressed him in cotton skirts and sleeveless sweaters that I picked out in secondhand stores, using only one criterion: each garment had to be exceptionally confiding. The life of its previous owner needed to have bled vividly into the fibers to compensate for whatever would go unsaid or undreamed of in the new wearer. I had to apply this criterion harshly, because the kid was warm but otherwise unwieldable. I knew enough not to expect much from him in the way of help around the house. But I enjoyed arranging myself into a chair he had just absented for another bath or his hourly shave. He kept the bathroom door locked behind him and took his time.

What was between us eventually got beneath everything.

THE GIST

She had nothing in common with her body anymore, was how she put it. Her body was going somewhere else.

A place? A direction? I was halfway curious. That winter, there was a lull between my legs that made it easier for things like this to come up. Plus it was bedtime. We were still in our clothes of the day, our work clothes.

I led her out to the car and made sure she got in. Then I got in on the passenger side.

I made her drive with the lights off.

"Show me where," I said.

At first she drove fast and sarcastically. You can get away with that in my state, because it gets so wide at night.

This was the second time I was on this wife, my second marriage to the same wife. Does it figure that neither of us had ever bothered to come up with any nicknames? When we talked, we had to use the same names everybody else had been getting away with using on us.

"I am at the point where," the wife began. For a while, all the talking was about points where. I pictured the points not as the loose, dotty kind but as the arrowy ends of things. This kept me occupied. Then came the parts that started with "As far as my life." Sometimes she remembered to say "is concerned."

"Keep your eyes on the road" was all I said whenever it came time for me to let her know that I was going along with what she was saying, the sticky gist of it. To be doing something, I looked out the side window, where rurality kept taking place in the dark.

When the sun came up, we got out and found jobs.

"Nobody is ever overqualified for this kind of work," the manager said.

He led us into a long room full of card tables. There was a folding chair at each table. The other people would not start showing up for at least another hour, the manager explained.

"In the meantime," he said.

We took turns doing what we were told.

THE PAVILION

I came up with a new angle on how to start a family, an entirely new way of going about the business of it, and went from place to place—parking lots and boardwalks, mainly—to talk up the talking points.

I had pass-outs, outgivings—*literature* was the word people liked. There was a fifteen-minute presentation and a forty-five-minute presentation, and, for some reason, the longer one always went over better. People wanted to stand through such things.

Afterward, men and women alike said, "We'll be rooting for you!" and "Keep us posted!" and "Are you from around here?" A few would hand me money— mostly folded fives. "Put this toward it," they would say.

I did my driving at night and slept mornings in the car. A shower curtain bunched up against the windshield kept out enough of the light. If I couldn't sleep, I shuffled through the little "To Serve You Better . . ." evaluation cards I often pressed on people at the end of the longer presentation, expecting phone numbers and addresses to have been squiggled out propositionally, but finding only "Could you maybe go a little more into the nuts and bolts of 'bypassing the problem entirely'?" or "What are you hiding?" Once, a man followed me all the way to my car and said, "You ever even been married?" I told him that I had once had a wife who adored me out of house and home.

Whether I slept or not, by noon I had already washed myself in the basin (I used bottled water and dish detergent) and was back on the road. I drove until I found a promising site. To get a crowd started, I set up my easel and paint set and theatrically slapped out a picture of the pavilion I had in mind. As I saw it, it was a steep-roofed substantiality with cinquefoils, observatories, anything. I threw in lean-tos and tented offshoots, castellar outbuildings with escalators. I had to people the grounds with peoply daubs, though, if I expected passersby to pause and gawp and chum me up. "What is that, exactly?" they would ask. Or: "Would it be an actual place?" Or: "Is it within a day's drive?"

One afternoon, I had everything assembled on an alleylike amusement pier that ledged out over a closed beach. After the crowd was gone, a girl stepped lankly toward me, her hair roughed up, her eyes slimed. She wore a smock of the most besetting blue—a blue I had often seen days acquire difficultly and never let go of without first kicking up a storm. There was a splashy adequateness to the big picture I was getting.

"Highest grade completed?" I asked.

"Some college," she said.

"Why just some?"

"Nobody was telling me anything. Plus all that underlining."

"Boyfriend?"

"No way of knowing."

"Your parents?"

"Still way too married."

"Brothers and sisters?"

"Two sisters."

"Older or younger?"

"One of each."

"What kind of girls?"

"The pep-talky kind. Two-faced behind your back."

"Complete this sentence: Here it must be said that . . ."

"Here it must be said I just want to get the duration over with."

Later that afternoon, while her smock was being dry-cleaned in town, we worked through the actual mechanics behind the shower-curtained windshield. I had the car parked on a stony crescent of beach. Afterward, I started writing simple booklets for her to read—nothing inspirational or fact-ridden, just whatever came to mind that would advance her from one interim to the next. "Busy books," she called them. "Write me another busy book real quick," she would say.

I had to piece together a diet for her, too. I knew which combinations of which foods on which days would rehang everything that was draped so delicately beneath her skin. In a matter of months, the body under the smock was organized anew, redistributed.

I gradually worked the girl into the presentations, both the short and the long ones, first as an assistant to hand out the handouts and point the pointer at the charts, then as a participant with a speaking part. When she started rounding out and the baby started showing through, I inaugurated a question-and-answer segment and put her entirely in charge.

There was really only one question, though, that the audience could ever think of to ask: "How come the baby seems to be riding so high on you? It seems up awfully high."

The girl's answer would always be: "I'm not sure I understand exactly what it is that's being asked."

Another person would give it a try, but in different words. There were only so many words an audience of any size could come up with. When they ran out, I would have to step in and say, "This is all very new to all of us." I would bring up the pavilion one more time. "Pavilions will take the place of homes as we know them today," I would say. I would go on about if and where the model pavilion would be brought to completion, what kinds of castered dividers would divide it into divisions, the color of the dyed burlap that would be stapled to the dividers as decoration. The girl would chime in with anything statisticky I might have left out—measurements, cost figures, and suchlike—then circulate the evaluation cards and the pencils.

Later, in the car, as I beat the girl's food together in the tureen, I would hear her turning the pages of the booklets in the back seat, biding her space. When I was finished, while she ate, I would try to sleep, curled up, on the roof.

Sometimes the girl cried all night as I drove. I would have to pull over every few hours and get in the back seat and put my arms around her. By this point, she was pronouncedly hump-bosomed. Where her tiny breasts had once reposed, there was the cyclopean, orbiculate business of the coming child instead.

Late one morning, the girl said, "I'm close."

"How soon?" I said.

"Within the hour?"

94

I drove to the biggest town within reach—it had a Euclid Avenue and a Fifth Avenue and a Market Street and a Wabash Avenue and a Pennsylvania Avenue—and parked at a dumpish shopping center. There was no time to set up the easel. I had the girl doped and laid out upside down on a chaise longue, her head where her feet would have ordinarily gone.

People started gathering. From a box in the trunk, I abstracted a handful of handouts for the fifteen-minute performance.

With a pliers, I gentled the girl's teeth from their sockets.

I dropped the teeth one by one into my shirt pocket.

"Otherwise," I said, "she's likely to bite the poor thing involuntarily."

Then the tongue.

I had to widen the mouth just a little at the sides.

When the girl started to gag, I reached into her throat and threaded everything out that was coming. The girl went blue in the face. I slapped her first, then the kid, then the girl again.

The two of them—and the crowd—were breathing loudly, busybodily.

I did my best to keep in touch with the kid and its mother afterward and repeated the process with a couple of other like-bodied girls up and down the coast, and in a few years I had become some kind of king, reigning over something noticeable.

PRIORITY

I keep changing my story when in fact it could not be more straightforward or plain. It is a story of none too many people, least of all me. But set me down where there is a bigger turnout and I am one minute picking somebody up, the next minute getting myself picked up—I have no heart for upholding the difference or keeping myself laden with the life of me even this far.

It is too much like work.

To wit, I found something of hers in the bathroom not long afterward—a Band-Aid that had never made its way to the wastebasket and, instead, dropped between where the side of the sink cabinet did not quite reach the wall. I was trying a final time to fish up a comb that had fallen down the same crack. The better comb—the clean one—was already packed. I was using a length of undershirt cardboard when the Band-Aid got dredged up. There was a blur of dried blood on the gauze pad. I am just assuming the blood was hers. I am giving her every priority.

Can we at least be in agreement that the things dicks perk out toward vary from one person to the next but are subject in the end to similar spoilage?

Because it is easy to forget that the Band-Aid is still in my wallet, smutted, souvenir-style, but who thinks to look? I never got the comb back, either. I had to use wet fingers to get my hair set aright. I drove across the state toward the house, the close-quartered sorriness, of my parents, talking to myself in an overconcerned announcer's baritone the whole tollway long. It was a voice instigated for letting on that the marriage had never sunk in. Whenever billboards appeared, I read them aloud just as elegiacally.

I stopped just once, at a place called A!D!U!L!T C!A!S!T!L!E. Eight booths, each about the size of a shower stall. The chink of belt buckles and the trinkle of pocket change as the pants came down, mine first; the dismal rumpus itself; then the dirt-colored paper towels—I kept moving myself about within one vast stickiness of long standing.

The same whole world was still waiting to get wiped.

My parents were of course glad to see me, glad I had some time off, glad they would not have to cross the street every morning for the newspaper. I would have the dime and quarter heating in my palm before I even entered the store.

My mother was free to fight arthritically with the neighbors about the noise. She sat in the breakfast nook and listened to the people on both sides warming to the day and the sounds assembling inside it. By noon, things would be organized, bulked, around a central, controlling disturbant—a power tool or stereo or spat. She would shout, make threats over the phone.

I dusted. Carried out more garbage. Tried to replace the doorbell. Afternoons, I did the marketing. The name of the checkout girl would get printed in pale-violet ink at the bottom of the receipt. The receipts accumulated in my pocket. I would reach into it for my keys and feel the girls feel the sudden extra weight on themselves. People could tell when they were being dwelled upon.

Nights, I put myself through conversation. There was a sister for the three of us to discuss. She had had two children so far, the boy and the girl. The boy kept everything to himself and did not want to be seen eating. The girl claimed she never ate.

"Bragging or complaining?" is all my father said.

I have no real way of knowing how many nights it took until a man my age let himself into the house and ventured steadily from room to room. He entered my parents' bed, saw how much space remained between the rims of their bodies, then fidgeted himself into it. In no time, he had a finger of one hand deep inside my mother, had my father's undertrousers pushed all the way down to the knees, had a finger of the other hand as far as it would go up the crack.

The idea must have been for it to become somebody else's turn to bring somebody else into a world.

RECESSIONAL

For the sake of argument, know everything about me.

I was a flask-shaped man in a velour shirt sitting at long lunchroom tables in business schools, cosmetology schools, junior colleges, community colleges. My business was buying used textbooks and crating them off to a distributor. Kids would come up and lunge their thick, thuddingly unread books at me. I would lip the names of the authors and the titles—Gurson's *Invitation to Secretarial Science* or Fritchman's *Accounting Principles Today*, third edition—and flirt through my blue loose-leaf price guide while the kids gloomed above me. Then I'd reach into the tackle box I kept my cash in, slam some dollar bills and quarters onto the tabletop, watch the hands grubble for the money.

I no longer even looked up at the knocking incoherences of the kids' faces, which were mostly acned rinds, fuzzed-over globes. Instead, I concentrated on their arms. In short-sleeve weather, especially, their arms were the most vocal parts, each one clarioning a need that had nothing to do with what the face might be asking for.

I never had to say a word, either. The kids never questioned how much I paid. They would just pivot around, happily disembarrassed, lunch-moneyed.

I'd been floating this version of myself for nine months in a three-state territory, paying off bills and piling lots of cash aside. I was on the road every other week. Each morning, in a motor-court cabin or motel room, the woman expertly folding everything in sight—starting with the special sheets and pillowcases I always brought along so I wouldn't have to fall asleep atop the heavily dreamed-on bedclothes provided by the motels, with their unbleachable residues of heart-scalded travelers—was never the woman I lived with. In each case, she was an unaired, hamsterish woman with a mouthful of loose fillings and certain thrilling agitations of speech. She had a flicky way with a pair of pants, my ice-cream pants, which she saved for last.

She had her grateful housekeeping-staff counterpart at every motor lodge on the map.

The man I was in each of those rooms with that woman or her equivalent was down to three hundred and twenty-five pounds in the mornings.

With her, my undecidable life was in remission.

I was losing my hearing. The words trending toward me in conversations often arrived pumiced, their meanings smoothed off, rinsed away. If I wanted, I could squint my ears toward the words and make out the gist, funnel them down to the threats and insults, the "You fat fuck!"s. But could I be blamed for preferring everything foamed over to a thwooosh?

Still, I kept the appointment that the woman I lived with had made for me with an audiologist, a no-obligation consultation. The audiologist was a pulpy blond. She bracketed a set of earphones over my skull, and I compliantly uncurled a finger and raised it each time I got a purchase on one of the fugitive tones she let loose in my head. Afterward, she graphed the cordilleras of my nerve deafness on a quadrille memo pad. She swiveled on her chair to get closer to me and, syllabizing exaggeratedly now, explained the test results. Then she corked a sample "hearing instrument" into my ear. I instantly reacquired the honk and slam of the world, only tinny and trebled, a clacking souvenir-soundtrack version.

Then I noticed what the audiologist was doing with her face—louvering it open and shut, open and shut. I'm not talking about blinking or a tic. There was nothing metronomic or involuntary about it. She was slatting her face closed and opening it for me again, shuttering out what she wanted me to know about her, keeping things safely unsyllabled but unmisconstruable.

It wasn't just this one woman, either. Lately, people had been flagging me with napkins at lunch counters, inclining menus toward me meaningfully. Morsing me with the rataplan of fingertips. Wigwagging their arms at me in clammy rush-hour crowds. Browing and swallowing vividly, declaratively, for my benefit. Worse, they expected me to get what all the sirening and signage added up to.

Everybody was a sexual emergency.

Once, in a department store, after witnessing some seizured semaphoring near a rack of summer shirts, I tagged after a man up an escalator and into a vaultlike restroom. We stationed ourselves in adjacent stalls. He cupped his palms against the metal wall and megaphoned, "Do you miss someone?"

I unlatched my door. He brisked his way in, a recklessness of chiaroscuroed forearms and a dank, rebusing face. He unhaunted me for five minutes tops. Then I junked him from my thoughts.

So what I said to the jalousie-faced audiologist was, "Let me sleep on this." I unstoppered my ear and set the demonstration model on her desk.

I watched her pull her face shut with a tantrummy tug.

Then I went home to the woman I lived with.

Gloria had three daughters by her ex-husband. She had provisoed from the start that a second marriage was out of the question, exactly what I had wanted to hear. The girls were espaliered on their mother—tamped down, battening on her. When I wasn't on the road, I ghosted parenthetically through their days. But I made an effort to figure those kids out. I did. I delved into them, parsing and plundering swatches of their fissured nervous systems. They had been through a lot, I reminded myself. I imagined that they had started out as tidy, exact quotients of their mother and their father (an amply brainsick, runaway refrigerationist named Sandy) and the things the two parents had said at the table—the household slang they had evolved for borborygmic high jinks and the like. Then Gloria and Sandy had begun farming out a large share of their hatreds, fractioning it among the three girls to see how much they could take and what they would work it into. And then the beatings, ambulanced trips to the hospital, hushful visiting hours by Gloria's intensive-care bedside, the daily hand-holding ceremonial walk to the hospital gift shop for candy. After the divorce, watching all the newcomers single-file in and out of Gloria's bedroom, the girls had resignedly rounded themselves off to the nearest full-time adult: their mother. They never mentioned their father. I am certain that during my absences my name never came up. Each of the girls despised me in a different, unexploded way.

Late one afternoon, returning from a weeklong book-buying trip and squattering into the living room, I found the three of them, batched and mumpish, on the carpet. The second-oldest was beached three feet from the dust-filmed TV screen, folded in on herself, thighs pressed against chest, crossed arms propped on the shelf of her knees, her thumb plugged into her mouth. All of this took place beneath a huge, tentlike T-shirt, one of mine, tie-dyed into Day-Glo swirls without my permission, the neckhole pushed up all the way to her nose, armless sleeves hanging limp.

The other two girls were idling on either side of her, still slung in the underwear they had slept in. I waded midway into the room, then halted, cantilevering my paunch above their heads.

"Hi, girls," I gargled.

No response.

Lineamentally, though, they were good kids—sparrowlike, blue-veined, each with an aureole of gingerish hair. My own face looked as if it had been sketched out as a shenaniganal exercise and then immediately, apologetically, scumbled over and shaded into something you could at least linger on without thinking, "Is he simple?"

I gave the contents of the TV screen, *my* TV screen, a distracted appraisal, then lobbed toward the stairs.

I knuckled on the bedroom door before entering.

I found Gloria in bed with a magazine and a cigarette, her hair still spongy from a shower.

"The girls came across that female-supremacy literature you ordered from that club," she said, dictioning each word as a favor to me but not looking up from the page she was on.

"Then shouldn't they be doing handstands?" I said. My voice was fat-clogged and remote. I couldn't even be sure my words had got all the way out.

Gloria shot me a stay-thither look and returned to her magazine. Unstuffing wads of bills from my pockets and slapping them onto the dresser, I watched her read, watched her eyes dartle across columns of type. She was a speed-reader, steeplechasing through more books and magazines and newspapers in a month than I managed in a year, and yet I was the one with the diplomas, the certificates, the letters of recommendation.

She had a strapping, hoydenish body. She maintained a sunlamped handsomeness. But she was hygienically delinquent. I wondered what my predecessors had made of the ashtrayish, perspiry nimbus she almost always hazed around herself.

I'd emptied my pockets. I flattened and stacked and justified the wads, trued them up for her approval. Then my eyes chanced upward at the mirror. I looked strewn.

"Did you eat? Are you hungry?" she said.

"I didn't stop anywhere," I said. The words fogged out of me.

"*Bluh-blub-bluh-blub-bluh-blub-blub*. Talk right. Jesus."

"I said no." I was forming the syllables slowly and effortfully this time. "I haven't eaten anything."

"The only reason I ask is that the girls are going to their aunt's. Somebody's coming over I'll need to be alone with."

"Who?"

"Who? Whoever. Go eat."

104

"No...I mean, just for the record."

"The record? All right: you know that checkout girl at Foodtowne, the one you're always carrying on about right and left? With the biceps? I've been fucking her all week as a goodwill gesture to you. It's an act of largess. There's no recreation involved, hardly. She asks about you all the time. Okay? Now go somewhere and eat."

My hands fisted as far down as they could go in my pants pockets. I stood there, a shadow-slopping, chronically howevering man in a room that sloped slightly toward an uncurtained window. An erection began to dumbly press itself out.

"Obey," she said.

"Look," I said.

But I wasn't pointing at anyone or anything. There wasn't anything for anyone to see.

To my credit, I knew which days were over. Days, for instance, when I could stump into any diner, canvass the menu, and, commanding the vocabulary of entrées, side dishes, and beverages, feel confident that the waitress scrabbling out my order on a guest check would understand everything that the Swiss steak, whipped potatoes, buttered noodles, chowchow, and orange juice stood for from my standpoint. Days when, minutes after the plates and dishes and tumblers had been arrayed in front of me, the waitress would reappear to ask, "Everything okay here?" and her words would pour out in a clear broth, and my "Yes, ma'am" would be weighted and epigrammatic, foreshortening the entire history of my lives in and out of women. After dessert, I would leave the diner satisfied that I had placed a rendition of myself in the waitress's memory for safekeeping: not the whumping, flagship version—crowding forty, flabbed over—that restroom mirrors kept serving, but a charitable likeness of the uncramped life I was conducting beneath the threshold of myself.

For months now, however, what I had been trying to get out and put across in public—not just in diners and coffee shops—had kept sinking deeper inside myself, blotted up in suety layers, dendrochronological rings that archived my departure from the world of speaking and listening. I was sealing myself in. When words did manage to spurtle forth, they wrenched off and garbled themselves surrenderingly in the air, finished with me.

My last time at a diner, a week or so earlier, I'd ordered Salisbury steak, parsleyed potatoes, and applesauce, but what the waitress set before me was a pair of crab patties, French fries, and coleslaw. When I fluttered out a yodelish, hyperventilated complaint, she bustled through her memo pad, unperforated a green-shaded page, and shoved it at me. On it were my booth number (17) and, in a dribble of misspellings and abbreviations, the order for the crab patties, fries, and slaw. "You don't see anybody else raising a stink, mister," she said.

But I was hungry. Leaving Gloria to her appointment with her Foodtowne girl, or whomever, I pursed my way downstairs and out to my van. My bags were still tossed over the heavy cartons of books in the back. I climbed in, turned the key, inched out of the hedgy suburb. I ramped onto the loop of parkways and bypasses that cinched in the city. I bucketed along beneath the speed limit, let myself be overtaken by homing secretaries and paralegals and telemarketers, all sleek in their toyish cars. I finally exited onto a service road and fell in with a vast taillit recessional notching past diners, family restaurants, cocktail lounges, fast-food dispensaries. I kept going until the garden apartments gave way to the warehouses and turreted row houses that husked around the battered downtown business district.

A couple of years earlier, when I'd miscooked myself into the guise of an employment counselor and reported each morning to a frontless, ribbon-windowed building off Center Square, I'd wambled away long lunch hours downtown. But I hadn't been back since.

I parked the van at a meter that still had seventy-five minutes left on it and started huffing the two blocks to McDonald's. Except for a few gibbering solitaires halted at crosswalks, I was alone on the overlit street.

Inside McDonald's, I humped down a long aisle of plastic booths in which offcasts from rooming houses roosted alone or in liverish confederacies, most fingering the barely sipped cups of coffee that entitled them to stay.

I fetched up, short-breathed, at the counter.

I watched a bulgy, sweat-sluiced man point to the wrapped hamburgers heaped behind the counter, then slowly, fatly, heft his index finger. I watched the countergirl ring up the sale and the man carry the hamburger, trayless, along with a couple of ketchup packets and a shock of fist-rumpled napkins, to a lone, tenuous table wedged near the side-street entrance. I watched him hunch into his seat and then whisk off the wrapping of the sandwich, jerk the beef patty from between the twin cushions of the bun, deposit it on a bed of napkins, and, with another napkin, strenuously wipe the ketchup, onions, mustard, and pickle from the underside of the bun's crown. I watched him turn next to the patty, first mopping up its sickly slather of condiments, then swaddling the meat between thicknesses of napkin and drubbing the grease out of it with his overfleshed fists. I watched him swab the pickle, shred it, then rain the fragments onto the patty. I watched him slit open a ketchup packet and gingerly squish out curlicues onto the meat. I watched him caliper the patty between the thumb and forefinger of each hand and lower it onto the heel of the bun. I watched him give the finicked, reconstructed sandwich a blunt-fingered tap.

I watched him venture a troubled lunette of a first bite, then hulk up from his seat, hamburger in hand, and take a few slow, expeditionary steps across the several feet of littered floor that separated his fastness from a trash receptacle. By this point, I guess everybody else was watching him, too—even an old black man, tenanting a booth close by, who until now had been gutturalizing contentedly, eyes shut, over the wreckage of a caramel sundae. Everybody had decided that this damp, widespread man with a hamburger was history in the making.

I watched him, only a step away from the trash receptacle, abruptly change his mind about jilting the sandwich. His thoughts friezed across his doughy face, every one of them an open secret. They were so clear, and they followed in such a tidy succession, that I could have written them down for later. Instead, I watched him prize himself back into his seat, guttle the rest of the hamburger in four or five bites, rear up again, then pant and swivet his way out to the street, leaving a snowdrift of napkins to be cleared away.

I watched him thump the two blocks to where his van was parked. That was when I got the feeling I was horning in.

That was when I was sure I had outstayed my welcome.

I watched him hoist himself into the van and drive off.

MINE

Do what I do: come from a family, have parents, have done things, shitty things, over and over and over. There was the one day I got too friendly with my friend. The next summer, I welcomed men into the house while my mother and father were at work. I did this to the exclusion of everything else I was cut out for at twenty-two. The men passed through me one way or the other and came out narrowly mine.

That was the one summer my heart had clout.

In the early evening, I would sit on the patio while my father stooped among his flowers. I could never sit for more than half an hour without having to get up to walk to the bathroom at least once. I don't know what I was expecting to come out, but I never once looked. I would put the lid down before I flushed.

Later, in the dining room, where the table would already be set, my father would say his piece. It always amounted to the same thing: if there was a problem, I should let Dr. Zettlemoyer know.

After dinner, I would go straight to bed. I crossed each night by linking one minute securely to the next, building a bridge that swung through the dark. I did my real sleeping in the morning sun, and around noon the first of the men would knock. The fact that they spaced themselves out assured me that they all knew one another and got along and were reasonable. Whoever was first was never a matter of surprise, but I think they would have liked the sequence to hold meaning.

My father never came home sick in the afternoon to find me on my knees in the living room with my mouth full of somebody's grave, helpless perpendicularity. I never got to see my father eye to eye like that, the only way I wanted to.

My father: what stood out about him was that his life got put past him.

It was my mother who taught me the one worthwhile thing: when they ask if you like what you see in the mirror, pretend that what they mean is what's behind you—the shower curtain, the tile, the wallpaper, whatever's there.

Steep

The gray bowl that my husband ate his cereal out of, the bowl he had brought to the marriage from someplace else, a bowl from which I had never eaten, did not break or chip or go back to where it came from. It simply stopped coming to the table. Up until then, events had been uneventful: I washed and dried the bowl, then returned it to the cupboard. The exertion involved was minimal—in truth, I welcomed it—but I screamed bloody murder every time.

I think I already know what comes next: a stipulative definition of marriage as an accidental adjacency of flesh in which small, unbegrudged exchanges of affection are fitfully possible provided that...and then you get so many pages of *provided that*s. The pages are wrinkled-looking, as if somebody had read them in the bathtub and then set them out on the floor to dry. The definition is the foundation of a vast, steep, plunging counterargument against which I am defenseless unless I spill two beans that I have been saving in my blood because what other privacy do I have? These two beans have been prowling in my blood for too long. The first bean is so simple, so obvious, that I have to work extra hard to keep putting it back into words, just to keep it in words: the woman he was seeing stopped letting herself be seen.

The second bean I have to condense. I woke up and he was biting my finger in his sleep. Not sucking—biting. An irksome switch, his being the container, instead of being gouged into *me*, slopping around inside when I was dead to the world or pretending to be. I was inside *him*. I was the one getting chewed up.

What I did was swack him on the head twice, three times. He eventually woke up. I told him what he had done.

He said, "Is that right?"

Because I was a woman he knew to speak to.

Ever since, the fundamental unit of discourse, the basic building block of speech, has been my mouth asking: "What's scarier than two people in a room with their nightstands and the things they keep on their nightstands?"

I make it sound as if I know an answer.

THE DAUGHTER

The man was afraid of heights, of looking up. This was well known around the house. It was a household fact.

It was well known that when the man went outside he wore a cap with a long bill that awninged off unreliable tracts of sky.

The daughter knew all this.

One day, the man walked into the kitchen, which was shooting up several stories and becoming elaborately, sculpturally, tiered and balconied. He kept his half-closed eyes trained low—on the countertops, the slats of the chairs. He found some semblance of his wife at the table.

"We need to look for another house," he told her.

The silence was more vertical than ones he was used to.

"Do you hear me?" the man said.

"You can hardly notice it," his wife said.

The man put on his cap and walked to the daughter's school to talk to her teachers. He watched their faces when he gave them her name.

"She never comes," is all the teachers would say. They each showed him a columned page of a roll book on which she had been checkmarked absent every day of the term.

"Describe the girl for us," one of the teachers said.

The man talked at reckless length about the daughter. The teachers complained that the more he talked about her, the less they could picture a girl or even the outline of what a girl might look like. They said that what he was talking about seemed more like a place, the capital of someplace, than a person.

"I'm not apologizing," the man told them.

When he got home, he left his cap on and panted up flight after flight of stairs to the daughter's room.

She was in bed, asleep. He looked down at her face, into her ears. He looked up her nostrils. In the left one he saw a stalactite of dried mucus. He left it alone. He sniffed at her underarms. He sniffed the entire length of one leg. He smelled her mouth. He gave it a spitty, plunging kiss.

A city was steeply taking shape around the daughter. The voluminosity of it made the man want to give up. He felt he had to see. He threw his head back and, clinching his tongue between his teeth to keep from swallowing it in fright, watched skyscrapers stunting overhead, crooking and curling, blousing out.

THAT WHICH IS HUSBANDER
THAN ANYTHING PRIOR

I stopped mistaking what the husband was doing for merely a new way of coming and going. I started regarding it as what it more likely was: a series of faultful, pestering steps taken farther untoward me. I had to adjust my own footing accordingly.

In bed, I kept my nose stuck in a book that listed pairs of words people often confused. It was something the husband had brought into the house early on, in a violent bout of furnishing. For instance: *intimidation* versus *intimation*. Only, I did not necessarily see where the versus came in.

I lived in a town that had sourceless light falling over it at all hours. At the front of the phone book, right after the dead-blue street map, came the claim that the town was within a so-many-mile radius of an immense fraction of the country's population. But every time I set foot on the streets, they withheld their longitude from me. They reneged on distance.

It was a town of meantime everlasting where, for homework, sheets of paper got numbered from one to fifty. The homework was unacceptable unless submitted in folders the teachers could drop off and pick up in the old metal milk box on my porch. The only time I had to meet the teachers was when they were new and thus understandably doubtful until I brought them into the bedroom, where they could see for themselves the picnic table with its jars of shining stick-pens, the banks of papers and folders, the bulletin boards shingled with teachers' handwriting samples and grade-inflation charts. Afterward, I would walk the teachers to the door, watch them tuck themselves into their cars.

In the folders, I would always find that some of the pages had been balled up and then sorryishly, second-thoughtfully, smoothed out. Others would be torn and flapped, pleated or petaled. Occasionally I came upon papers that had been soaked and crinkled and fancifully dyed or shaded until there was something cabbagy about the results. The greater number of sheets, though, arrived with coatings, toppings—not just spilled coffee and soda, smeared chocolate or pizza, but rampancies, offscourings, of the body. Often, opening a folder, I would be greeted by the concentrated smell of underparts preserved with uncanny loose-leaf fidelity. Whatever the students could get out of themselves, they put on paper for whoever collected. "Hand something in," I could hear the teachers saying.

Before the husband who kept leaving left for good, he accused me of two things: hirsutism and "self-dependence." It is true that I had hair scribbled fine-pointedly over my arms and the backs of my hands and a few other places. It is also true that I liked to keep the marriage almost entirely to myself. There was more to get out of it that way.

I started keeping the hair sleeved out of sight but went to doctors about the rest of the body, because it was not tiding me over. It did not suffice. There was the general practitioner who wanted to overcome his disinclination to heal just long enough to help me retain what I slept, because by morning all of it got away from me. And the neurologist: she was the only one I could think of to go to about the commotion in my face, the twitch that made my cheek blink separately from my eye. But it was the dentist I visited the most. He filled my cavities, the same ones, again and again, each time with something different: artful arrays of streaming silk threadlets, cleverly tinctured plasters and slurries, crystals whose enchasement could take hours. By the time I left his office, my tongue was already working the fillings loose, and everything would get swallowed later in my unbottoming sleep. In the morning, I would stare in the mirror at my rows of teeth—the slanting, headstony front ones, especially— until I found the holes. I would drive to the dentist and let him put his hands back in my mouth. I would go home afterward and put my own hands in places that did not have as clear an opening.

It was soon after that—after the marriage and the appointments—that I started the invitations. In one folder, I found a sheet on which was typed, red-ribbonly, "Every floor your on, is somebody elses ceiling, step lightly, please, show some feeling." This was biology, the science of life—a lab report for the junior college. I looked at the name: Lu Clovis. I looked down at my hand, which, at the foot of the page, was already writing: "I'm not the teacher." Beneath that, I gave my suppertime whereabouts, the name of the restaurant, for the week ahead. I pictured what they called the "nontraditional student": a housewife on the brink. But she showed up young, maybe twenty-three,

118

and incompletely clean. She let a collapsible umbrella spill onto the table before she sat down. Her hair was brown and streamy. She had a forward body building up toward something already. She wanted to know where my youth had gone, how long at current address, what I had to go by, which people I held my life against, reasons for leaving whatever I might have left. But when I started to give her a factish rundown of some sort, keeping my palms up, hair-enshadowed sides down, her eyes went right out. I shut up and ate my sandwich until they came back on. They were brown, dry, blinking fast.

"I read that people who work at home put on suits just like people who commute," she said. The gutter above her lips—the downspout that there's a name for; it was in the book of pairs: *philtrum* versus *philtre*—started getting trickly with sweat.

"In my case, no," I said.

"I'm pissed," she said. Then: "Not about that. I'm here for something else, simultaneously or something. This is my fault—all right? I'm entitled? This is forgotten? This doesn't have to go down in memory? Excuse."

One thing led to another when there was no reason for the advance. Days were something I had to put myself into, regardless. There was no getting around where they were going.

In another of the folders, I found an over-epigraphed Child Psych term paper with the research broad and abundant at one end and, at the other, following a blank page, this: "I TAKE MY DAY ONE LIFE AT A TIME, I LIVE MY LIFE ONE TIME A DAY, ALONG THESE LINES MY BODY WILL ONE DAY WANT MY LIFE ON IT."

Below that was an exorbitant red signature that flamed out only after repeated bursts of paraphs and descending curlicues. The name was Tracy Frick. I did the "I am not the teacher" business again.

Because at home my bed was outdoors and amphitheatrical and, by this point, open to the public. Or because the husband, when there had been one in place, had run his finger up my leg as if untracing everything along the way, putting anything else in place of what was already there.

Look: here was folder upon folder full of words issuing from one aghast organism after another. The folders were in my house, in the room where my bed should have been. Which is why the bed was where it was and why I wrote what I wrote to a girl named Tracy, who showed up.

Only, Tracy was a boy—not even that, actually: just a display of height and posture. An unparentlike adult had followed him at a plausible distance, a woman with a squeezed, prevailed-upon face who boothed herself close by and now and then disappeared, a fresh cigarette skewed into her mouth, in the direction of the restroom.

I watched Tracy make a ketchuped muddle of his sandwich. His cheeks were stippled with acne—tender pimples that made me think of baby corn. We ate in swallowy silence.

Then he spoke.

"Is it possible to get away with talking about certain people as if they were far more distant, far more farther off, than they actually are?" he said. But this was already a speech—his eyes were nowhere near mine. "I ask this because I have been looking for a basis on which to talk about exactly one person. I have been imagining this basis as something plinthlike. The plinth would have to be high enough so that people walking past could not be sure who was doing the talking."

I looked over at the woman in her booth. Her hands were doing as much as they could with a paper napkin, trying to get it to the point where it was anything else but.

I entered into partial, tentative cahoots with her.

From here on in, I am speaking as someone with a sleeping disability—someone whose sleep, when it comes, is disabling to herself and others.

The last folder I ever graded was full of what looked like conjugations—page after page of permutational wordliness that struck me as overpostponed progress toward a second, fuller language. I red-penned the usual invitatory sentences at the end.

The man who days later sat down opposite me in the restaurant explained that he had a houseful of daughters who no longer wanted to be seen with him. He was many years my senior and loomed against himself in a way that was hard on the eyes. There was his body, which for some reason did not get the picture, and then there were its retractions, which, he said, had names and rooms and crawl spaces and undivided attentions of their own, and which poor-mouthed him, day in and day out, in notes magneted to the refrigerator.

The man had his bearings and was polite. I got him to go over his marriages, which had all been wide of the mark and not to his liking—spotty, topical impromptus set against a larger and larger landlessness. Between bites of his food ("The meal of the day," he called it), he tried to bring me around to where he claimed to be, which was the place from which you could see that between where the skin separating one body from another stops and where the air begins there is a place where nothing much should have to take place.

I said either "Ever?" or "How so?"

I was not keeping track.

It later turned out that I did not marry this man off the top of my head—there was no marriageable surface left on him that I could see—but when he got up to leave, most of me likely followed suit.

PEOPLE ARE ALREADY FULL

I was down to just two, the two of them, the two I had left.

It will be both convenience and courtesy—and I am hardly the one to overlook, as well, the pronominal luxury I will enjoy—if I make them, just this once, a woman and a man; but in actual, inadvertent life, you are sure to understand, they both were men—men of similar setbacks and altitude.

The man: I had to drive practically a week to reach him. My car niggled away at geography. The days were wide.

When I got there, the town was up against a bay. The slim streets were neither gridded nor ranked.

Later, on his terrace, he did not want me to call them photographs, and I did not want to call them merely pictures before I had a look at them for myself.

"Snapshots," one of us must have said, because by then the first of the albums was already being reckoned onto my lap. On each page, a listless, imperfect suction barely held the prints in place behind the clear plastic sheets. Toward the end, there were just glaring stacks in envelopes.

The depictions were last straws, old hat.

When it is two men—I still insist, I'll keep insisting—the one body disputes the other. What you see is one of them playing itself down, throwing off most of its weight, averting itself.

The pictures! A lot can happen if you stay awake, is all I ever got out of the things people kept shoving in my face and expected me to make instant snotty comments about.

But I elaborated myself into his arms: he was still a way for me to get a better grip on my body.

As for the woman? She lived in a city. Not the great scarped one you're right away imagining, but one that interferes with its inmates a lot less flatteringly. I wanted to know what she was doing up so early.

She explained that the moon operates on you for only so long, and then it stops and you're your own.

"Are you dry?" I said. "I am."

There was a cabinet on legs—not an ice box. The woman reached in and deducted some drinks, warm juice in cups.

I had to follow her to the sofa out of rude habit.

Until somebody tells me different, I am saying only that people are already full. The most you can do is lay yourself out on top.

THE PREVENTER OF SORROWS

At some point I played up to myself long enough to be living in a room that was scarcely part of the house it was tacked onto. Mornings, the open space between the bottom of the door and the carpet admitted a scalene wedge of light from more substantial regions of the house. Things besides light could have got in. It was my fault for not having insisted on a door that locked.

My troubles in the room were in fact few. I was living cajoledly as a woman. I worked in an office and was on concise, finite terms with the men I mixed with. I gave certain of the men permission to hunt and peck.

My thoughts at the time are said to have concerned proximity. Transportation was abundant. There was always a bus coming.

The properties of rooms are sometimes said to differ from house to house. I once rented a room in a row house on a through street. The room, it was insisted, was a convenience by which some extra, unruly space had been rectangled off to enclose someone for whom carnalities had become moot. By this point my lovers no longer recognized me on the paths along the river. They passed me with packages under their bare arms. I never managed much rest. The cubed air of my room hardened into a medium resistant to the through-passage of sleep. I could pat the air where it hung above my head.

How secure should you ever feel about anything that might go up on a wall?

For a time, I found that whenever I was on a street, I looked at people until I saw one who looked the way I expected the person to look who could put a room in my favor, bring it around to me.

I am speaking horribly again of where I was young.

It was a room in which the reception of articles, effects, was incomplete. I had been keeping to myself for months when a girl appeared to help me straighten things up. She did not think highly of herself. I hated to see her have to touch anything. I had to stop her fingers each time they were about to reach whatever should have been belonging only to me.

I convinced the girl that what I needed most was that she keep me company while I did the actual cleaning. This arrangement continued, awkwardly, for weeks. I was more and more beholden to the girl. One night I noticed a change. It was not a matter of light, of the turning of seasons. The girl had a new history on her—a different clutch on things. She had been admitted to the room: I could see her life coming down on her all at once. My possessions were now massily hers.

The woman was a stickler for partnership. She was smitten with better things to do. I followed her across an areaway and through an anteroom and into the room where the husband was already fixed up. The woman's face was narrow and red again. I could smell the deodorant on all three of us. The woman achieved her smile. That being so, I wiped my feet.

"I'm just starting out," I reminded her.

She touched my arm, as if to say: "That would be lying."

In return, I felt pushed.

I heard the door close behind me like before.

In time, the husband and I had everything packed into boxes and had the boxes piled high against the wall, leaving the center of the room clear. The husband stretched himself out on the floor. There the similarities should have had to end.

Something goes terribly wrong with a room when it has held only one life for a long time. I had been over this and over this with people who claimed otherwise. There was a room of mine that was looked at and taken the wrong way. I opened this room to a man who was bringing up girls his wife had already had. The girls became raucous, cocky explorers of my bed. I tried to level with them.

I was the new girl, the trainee. They had me behind the register. My room was across the street. The manager was driving at something.

"Drop all idea of this being a cake job," I saw him saying.

"Don't think that the things people line up on the belt spell something out. There is no 'whole other life.'"

I remember an attic room to which I brought sackfuls of used clothing from thrift stores, rescue missions. The clothes were complicated by the lives of the people who had worn themselves onto them. In each case, something of the wearer had worked itself into the fabric and defeated the detergents and bleaches. It was often the least celestial thing.

I did not draw the line at underapparel. I did not limit myself to what had been worn by men. There was a boxful of maternity dresses and another of maillots. There were children's sunsuits, snowsuits.

I never found opportunity to wear most of the clothes but arranged ways for them to impinge upon me outnumberingly. I slept beneath enormous odorant piles. The clothes pressed their way into the upper reaches of my sleep.

Dressed, I could feel myself spoken for.

There were men throughout the city to whom infants of a certain age had to be brought at least once a week. It was said that there were never enough of these men at any one time. Once, I ran into one of them on his way to his room. There was a woman at his side who did all the talking. I forget whether I was expected to do anything spectacular on her behalf.

The world was one place, and then, overnight, it became someplace else. This was brought about without a significant redistribution of landmasses or weather, without any change in the vocabulary people had to fall back on when asking for admittance.

I taught myself to live in water.

SLEEVELESS

I've had things in my eye, sometimes too many at one time.

Except this once.

It was during a standstill in some otherwise eventful unemployment on both sides. My wife was asking for permission. She was sleeveless. The car was already in her name.

"Let me at least have a look at him," is all I said.

He was waiting in a booth at a coffee shop. My wife slid in beside him. I don't ordinarily drink coffee, but he ordered it for all three of us. I was going to count the number of sips I took.

"This isn't my day," he said. He told us what had happened on his way over—near misses, thumbnail bios of the principals, etc.

We sat in the misorderly, picayune midst of my wife.

I let him butter me up. I tapped my foot on his. Just a tap.

Because I know myself from somewhere, surely.

I've been within an inch of my life.

There are no big doings in my heart that I know of.

I Am Shy a Hole

I hate it when it gets all languaged around like this. I don't want it to be "If I had a dog" or "If I don't have a dog." What concerns me is how to get it past the point where I can decide whether I want to do anything next.

In other words, this is always going to be about my mine, not yours.

Last night he told me we could narrow it down to a boy-girl thing, and I let him disrobe me. I had to think about the knees of the girl I sat across from last year in school.

This much is figured out: the thing about being a girl is that stuff is stuck inside you—but with a boy, stuff goes away and never comes back. A boy keeps losing himself. A boy just keeps watching himself run out. How much should this explain?

That *boy* is open wide at one end so things can make their way out? (Say it and you will never hear it stop until you make believe there is something else your voice could be for.)

Girl is shut tight: say it and it's already done away with.

None of this is in my face.

I am always saying *boy*, no matter what people think you hear.

CONTRACTIONS

When I was an old-enough kid, I prepared an exhibit of things I wasn't supposed to know—things my parents had done before they got married to each other. It was almost like a science fair: posterboard displays, Styrofoam props. I had been secretly working on the project for months, excavating most of the facts I needed out of spavined shoe boxes at the back of my parents' closet, and early one Saturday night when my parents and sister went shopping, I set everything up in the basement, mostly on the Ping-Pong table but overflowing onto the washing machine and dryer. The centerpiece was a four-paneled entry titled "My Mom Was Married Before, and I Have a Stepbrother I Have Never Met." Among the evidence arranged beneath cellophane was a mildewy set of Gregg shorthand manuals, each opened to a flyleaf on which my mother's spiderish, inwrought handwriting spelled out her first name and a rude-sounding, unfamiliar surname and then a month, a day, and a year before I had been alive. I had also put lots of work into the diptychs "*Another* Stepbrother of Sorts: Daddy's Secret By-blow" (I provided a dictionaryish sidebar, as well as photocopies of the legal papers detailing the terms of the settlement) and "The World of My Sister" (featuring a time line ticking off the five and a half months between my parents' St. Patrick's Day potluck wedding and my sister's birth). Breaking up the Magic Markered text were Xeroxed family snapshots I had shaded with colored pencils and captioned destructively.

I spent the night out with the kid who considered himself my boyfriend—a gripless Puerto Rican who always had an unlit cigarette slanted apostrophically into his mouth. At the kitchen table the next morning, I found my mother looking unslept, tear-swollen. My father was administering to his bare forearms the same slow sequence of slaps, brushes, fingertaps, and hair-tugs that years earlier I had decided added up to his stab at a formula for making himself disappear. My sister, however, was the one who was missing.

The upshot was that I eventually turned twenty-eight and found myself married. I fumed and soured and stenched in bed beside a husband who himself was a cloud of exhausts and leakages. Sleep became a contest: by morning, whose smell would prevail in the room?

My husband's piss drippled out day and night, slavering through his underwear, blurring the crotch of every pair with a corona of orangey yellow. He had an enlarged prostate, and he kept a plastic ice-cream tub beside the nightstand. Every five minutes or so until he fell asleep, I would hear him, sodden and unfaucetable, bowing and curbing himself along the edge of the mattress, the tub in one hand, the other jigging his penis against the inner rim until a driblet or two finally plipped surrenderingly against the plastic. Sometimes, after he had resettled himself in his zone of the bed, I would reach across and pat his slobbering penis. My hand would come away clammy, vinegared.

I had always been struck by how other people spoke so casually and unembarrassedly about their beds, as if a bed were merely an unshaming final destination on the day's itinerary. When I first lived alone, I thought of my own bed as a softer, more expansive version of a toilet, a fixture on which things got discharged or unrecoupable selves got squeezed out, then flushed away in cleansing eddies of the sheets. Later, when I began making myself available to others, every body that trespassed on my bed left behind a new, unfillable furrow in my mattress. Some were more like clefts, gougings. In college, I had had a roommate whose bed I one day stared at too long. The roommate had gone home for the weekend without having made her bed. I stared at the swirls and crests of the waved sheets and the bedspread. I felt their tidal coaxings. I was determined not to get up from my own mattress, where I was lying with one hand wound around one of the cold metal legs, and dive onto hers. I could hear the siss of showers in the lavatory down the hallway. I had probably already missed lunch. I contented myself with the explanation that what was playing across my roommate's bed was simply the afterswell of a certain kind of sleep, a slopping, heavy-going sleep that had excluded me *unslightingly*. My roommate had left a sweatshirt lying on the floor, and that was what I ended up wearing all day. It was the day I went up to a boy I had never talked to before and asked where he came from.

I had to buy things—little things—several times a day: tweezers, permanent markers, newspapers. With every purchase, I should have stood in a fixed, unambiguatable relation to the person behind the cash register, but the transaction almost always got complicated by the accompanying thermal exchanges, the glancing flesh of palms and fingertips as payment was tendered, change dealt out. Some days when I counted on these seductions, all I would get was a clerk who slammed the coins onto the counter or trayed them atop bills he then let parachute onto my outstretched palm.

I would rock an empty shopping cart back and forth in the aisles of stationery departments, notebooks and thick packages of filler paper cliffed on either side of me. Sometimes I would reach for a coilbound themebook and riffle the pages, unsticking them, vaguely sickened by the washed-out pink and blue of the margins and ruled lines. I would picture the prongy, unparallel outlines onto which teachers were going to drape unmemorizable facts.

Mostly what I wanted to find was a special piece of chalk like the one my third-grade teacher had always used to mark our positions on the linoleum floor of the stage. It was a sausage-shaped cylinder of soft chalk swaddled in flocky wool. Back then, I had wanted my words to stream out as smoothly and as scrapelessly as the lines and circles and X's that flowed from that overscaled piece of chalk. Instead, everything I said or wrote seemed to scratch something else out of the world. On tablet paper and on blackboards, my letters were bony and tined. I begged classmates to recopy my homework for me so that each answer would come out curved, clawless, quieted down.

I'd had a friend once. For years, our goosefleshy lives had abutted in classrooms, on playgrounds, at library tables. Even when we outgrew the stage when we could jungle-gym across each other's legs and trunk and arms, I kept piling my life beside hers. Once, an overclouded July afternoon when we were both thirteen, we were lying in a weedy field behind a shopping center. I managed to land my head on her belly and listen to the guggle and burble inside her. My ear was pressed against the bare skin between the hem of her T-shirt and the waistband of her shorts. She let out a laugh. It was a flat-voiced laugh, but it made my life seem suddenly solvable, performable. I started thinking about unpillowing my head and letting my hands balustrade up her long arms until our faces were close together, and that was when she jerked away. The fleshy suction of my ear against her skin, the vacuum between us, broke. She hunched up, propped her chin on her knees, began tugging blades of crab grass out of the earth. I hunched up, too, and looked at her. Her shins were hatched and shaded with darkish hairs that I liked because my blond ones were uninsistent, practically invisible. "What are you looking at?" she said. "Nothing," I said. But the next time I saw her legs bare, a couple of weeks later, they were razored, girled-up.

Late every night, my husband watched a black-and-white 1950s variety show on a nostalgia channel. Eyes shut, shoaling in some puddly near-sleep, I would listen to the splashes of applause and the effortful laughter of the live audience. Inevitably, a member of the audience, usually a man, would let out a sudden, petitioning laugh, a laugh out of sync with the lilt of the jokes. I found that I had to assign the man a face and mete him out a life as unfinishable as my own before I could shark off into sleep.

Once, returning home from work, I found my husband kneeling raptly before a wicker hamper from which my dirty laundry had overspilled. He was bobbing for my socks, incisoring into them one at a time, then craning around, depositing them onto the carpet, tandeming them off. There were already at least half a dozen heel-soiled pairs, each a different shade of off-white, laid out intently. His hands, meanwhile, were making slow, winging dips in the air around his cock, now and then grazing it as the angle of its levitation shifted.

I backed my way unnoticed out of the room. In the kitchen, I settled myself squeaklessly onto an upholstered chair. I thought about the sad, outcropped, lavatorial world of men. I had once met a man, a limericky professor, whose secret, unairable life's work was a definitive atlas of women's body-hair distributions: an oversized, plywood-covered volume, full of thick, eraser-pinked pages, that he kept clamped shut under a terraced heap of accordion files in the trunk of his car.

Men wanted my toes in their mouths or my torso roped against a chair or my mouth lipsticked and wordless or my brain ligatured to whatever unknottable neural twist that in their own brains winched their rawing, blunted dicks into place. It was always just one thing they wanted, or could handle, at a time. I had myself convinced that I had so many lives recessed inside me that I could afford to portion my body out part by part and not miss anything, that everything would grow back.

But I had a hard time finding anything even marginally fetishizable about a man's life. I would grub through my husband's nightstand and bureau-drawer dross—the siltage of receipts, business cards, watch straps, and crease-blurred newspaper clippings that shadowed him securely into the apartment. I would poke my finger through the front slit of a pair of his jockey shorts before I tossed his wash into the machine. I would stand in the bathroom and stare at the pepperish encrustation of his whisker-hairs in the unscoured sink.

Eventually he stopped haranguing me with sex altogether.

The only way in and out of the building where I lived with my husband was through a dim lobby furnished with a sofa, a card table, and some folding chairs. Coming and going, I had to walk past a pair of plaid-dustered old women who early each morning organized themselves onto the sofa and kept watch. Each had a cathedral of yellowish-gray hair whose bobby-pinned buttresses and pinnacles the other would frettily oversee. Gangling through the lobby, surveilled, I would occasionally let an unlipped, falsetto "hi" butterfly out of my throat and into the nets that the women's squeeching hearing aids unreeled into the dead air. But the women never even nodded. It was real work to operate my body past them, my life beating down on me with every step. It was even harder when I was dragging women in and out, one at a time, never the same one twice, during roiling, elongated lunch hours. Because by this point I had to have women, their knee-shine and susceptibilities, even though every one of them left me staled, depopulated.

Every year for six weeks in gym—a whole marking period—we had had what the teacher called "apparatus": monkey bars, parallel bars, the pommel horse, the high bar, the stationary rings. The teacher was a loudly married snoop with blunt legs duckpinning out of the same sort of salmon-colored trunks we were all required to wear. She knew I couldn't do a forward roll, which was the prerequisite to all other stunts, so she confined me to a special mat. Twice a week and for forty minutes at a time, I was supposed to kneel on that gashy, eraser-soft mat, tuck my head between my legs, and wait for a somersaultic force to exert itself on me and overturn the cinder-blocked gym and loop me forward into the same world everybody else was living in. But I remained untumbled, earthbound. Through the triangled space between my thighs, I would watch the spoked bodies of my classmates as they spiraled down the matted trackway that led to the apparatus, blazing their legs at one another. Then I would watch them skin the cat or stick-arm their way along the parallel bars.

On my mat, singled out, looked after, I bowed obediently into my groin and developed an overacquaintance with the inletted, divulgent body I presided over.

I started spending lots of time in my car—a rust-mottled, incognito beige Chevette. It was suddenly the room I felt most at home in, and it had enough of a sick-bay look to it to be thief-proof. The passenger-side leg well was table-solid with a pile of sallowing unread newspapers, and the crumb-strewn passenger seat made a companionable, multipurpose side-surface. I kept some extra cups and a box of plastic forks, knives, and spoons hutched on the dashboard. The radio gave out nothing but static, but it was the deep, bearable variety, not the kind of organized insect-kingdom roar that always brought on headaches.

After work and on weekends, I drove, rivering through the city and the suburbs. For a while I ate nothing but tiny meteorites of fried chicken that came casketed in clumsily slotted and tabbed cardboard. The arm that angled out of the drive-through window to hand me my box was almost always the same one: fuzzy, overbraceleted. It was an arm I wanted to have something to do with. Instead, the window would shut. Back on the service road, I would molar down the crumplets of chicken and let the grease terror through my system.

The women I was seeing were becoming less disappearable, and some started having names. There was Karen, a pharmacist with straw-blond hair and an asterism of nipply pimples that, during the days or hours I spent away from her, seemed to belt across her face zodiacally, never coming to a rest on one cheek or the other. The one with the chopped hair and paper cuts was Marcia: she drove a UPS truck. Dianne worked at an electrolysis studio. The waiting room would always be full of sleeveless young men hovering behind fashion magazines, and she would lead me upstairs to her uncurtained efficiency apartment, where she talked about her incumbent boyfriend and about the two other men who were after her and about how she was getting drummed out of her life. Gretchen was the one who kept saying she lacked the courage of her contradictions. She was afraid of losing her job at the community college because she didn't flatter the students enough. Each of these women was an exclamation of salty, spoiling flesh.

I came home every night. I would hurry through the underlamped lobby, ride the elevator to the third floor, find my husband on the living-room sofa. By this stage of the marriage, he had precipitated himself so exhaustively into the apartment that the air was urinous and unparting. Every room was snary with his life. His sleep trellised over towel racks and chair arms and shoe trees. It filamented from the handles of coffee mugs and the pocket clasps of mechanical pencils. Sometimes I would wake him and point to the bedroom. As he slippered past me, I would see his life training behind him, floor-fouled and unlanguaged, littery bits of myself magpied and particled into it. I still slept in the same brinkless bed with him. I would want to get up and shut off the candescence of the white shirt he had hangered to the closet door for work the next day, its collar pennanting in the breeze of the electric fan he ran as a noise filter.

My life had started to pill. I was fuzzing out little balls of myself that people would come up and twist off and flick into the already overpacked air.

At stoplights, I began to slope my neck sidewise so I could glint into whichever car was laned beside my own. The bloodshot, circumstantial desolation of the windowed faces—the splather of fingers against a cheek—was how I wanted things: wrung out.

I started wearing shopgirlish shirtwaists so that when I drove to the malls after work, I could be certain that if I lingered long enough at a display, restacking saucepans or arranging a strew of shoe boxes into a neat row, one old woman or another would eventually ask, "Miss, where would I find...," sealing off her question by salivaing the name of some unfamiliar-sounding kitchen utensil or sewing-box instrument. Her gaspy mouth would be a burrow of caries and glazed tongue. I would do my best to crease my face into blank lines and busy my hands menially with the merchandise before me. "You don't work here?" the woman, unanswered, would continue. I would wait until I no longer felt her stare singeing my cheek, then watch her flutter off toward a real salesclerk.

People in malls had it coming to them—even the girls wristing one another along from store to store or willowing about in a subjunctive sulk. The girls all had their lives marqueed brightly on their faces. My eyes would dart straight to their skirted legs, the flesh that glowed above the cuffs of their socks. Their skin was a threat.

A few blocks from the memorial park where my mother was staying put was a convenience store where I one day decided that the man behind the counter knew what he was doing. He kept an old metal dustpan on the counter. If you wanted to buy something, he pointed noncommittally to the dustpan, and sooner or later you figured out that he expected you to put your money on it, which you then did. He would grasp the dustpan by the handle and set it atop the cash register. He would ring up the sale, drawer the bill you gave him, plink your change onto the grooved ramp of the dustpan, and shovel the change toward the very edge of the counter, toward you.

This made sense.

It was a Saturday afternoon, early. What I bought was a stapler, a cheap blue plastic one, for my car.

ONESOME

To get even with myself on behalf of my wife, to see just how far I had been putting her out, I began to ingurgitate my own seed. I had to go through with everything twice the first night, because it came out initially as thin as drool and could not have possibly counted as punishment. The next time—I had let an hour or so elapse—some beads of it clung to a finger, and a big, mucousy nebula spread itself into the bowl of my palm. By the time I got everything past my lips, much of it had already cooled, but I revolved the globules around in my mouth slowly, deservedly, several times before allowing myself a swallow. There turned out to be nothing clotty or gagging about it— why, then, her gripes, her grudges?—just a bitter stickiness that stuck with me.

I repeated everything in the morning before work and again before bed. I began to hear—or imagine—a glueyness, a tightness, in things I now said. It made me think twice about opening my mouth.

Is it news to anybody that my wife had already given up on me hand and foot? She wanted her own room, and she got it, the small one downstairs we had never settled on any lasting purpose for. I went along, knowing how little it takes for a room to become the opposite of room.

Let me ask myself something else: should a father and his daughter have to fear each other tit for tat? Did I not make sure the door to her room was open when I made polite bedtime conversation with her? There was a prolixity of purple-blue veins legible beneath her skin, and on her face I could see my own features garbled, corrected, redressed. Childhood had cumulated in her and was getting ready to sour into something far worse. She had her own secret life and a circlet of friends who all had nearly the same name—Loren, Lorene, Lorena, I could never get all of them straight. She was a decent kid—picked up after herself, got high marks in the hardest subjects. I had no bone to pick with her except that she kept breathing down my crotch and then expected me to provide the food, the clothing, the shelter she needed to rule me out for good.

Marriage is what—the most pointless distance between two points? Or the foulest? Which?

My earlier marriages had all had a ring of adultery to them, because they were concise but inexact. For a long time afterward, I still looked in on the women in the supermarkets where they shopped, but we kept out of each other's eyes. I eventually saw every one of them vehemently pregnant—they deployed their bodies to brilliant effect for the men who came after me—and I was always on the verge of sending well-wishing cards with notes attached. But I kept my mind on getting in good with myself and watering down what I wanted from people.

Now I had another wife, and a daughter, to both of whom I was the last person on earth. I have already said everything about the daughter. But the wife, my last one: she was the one I married because how else this late was I going to get an idea of how many things a person did during the course of a day and then make sure I was doing the same number of things—only different ones, to keep me from looking too dependent? I could be civil to this wife once I knew her plans for the day, once I had an inkling of how much work was cut out for me.

Whatever my wife did, I would come up with something collateral, an equivalent. I would keep pace with her—chore for chore, personal occasion for personal occasion. Except that everything she did fell inside the marriage and everything I did fell anywhere but. I was no good at holding it in.

Example: two nights a week, my wife volunteered with a program that reached out to people for whom speech had become a hardship. These included the people who said *they* instead of *he* to jack up the population of their private lives. The county college offered a course the same two nights. It did not apply to the source of my livelihood, which shall remain nameless, but I signed up for it and bought the book. A girl sat next to me for weeks before finally markering "How are you fixed for people?" on a page of her thick semestral notebook. She tore out the page, folded it, filliped it toward me.

I wrote back what—that I am people-proof, a onesome?

A story can go on only so long before it stops being a joke.

It was a three-hour class with a fifteen-minute intermission that the prof kept postponing until later and later because nobody but a handful of studious

144

illiterates hung around for what followed. One night, at the start of break, the girl pointed out the window at a car that was a black oblong on the parking lot.

In the car, she said, "Guess what I cooked for supper—it stank up my hair."

I sampled a shiny hank of it in my fingers but could not place the smell. She drove me to somebody's house. We stationed ourselves at opposite ends of the living-room floor. When we both saw that that was all there was going to be to it—that just because there is a place for something doesn't automatically mean it belongs there—she drove me back to the lot where my car was.

I told everything to my wife.

Who wouldn't have?

She tracked down the girl by first name alone—called the registrar's office in one of her voices—and barely made trouble.

I called the girl just once after that.

"I know we had a falling out," I told her.

I went to grocery stores, expecting to find her buying further things to cook.

My teeth started sticking to everything I took bites from.

One morning, I could not get out of the house. I tried all of the doors and a couple of the windows. It was as if they were pasted shut. I turned on the radio, expecting nothing but static or long lists of school closings, but there was music, music with words rising from it familiarly.

I had to call off sick.

I looked at my wife, my daughter. One or the other said something about being hungry for something substantial.

I watched my wife reach into a cabinet for a frying pan. I watched my daughter open the refrigerator door. I duly unloosened myself from my chair. I started off in the direction of the silverware drawer.

I went on with their life.

For Food

He was a head taller than I, but he had arrived, midlife, at a way of scheming himself downward as he walked, of wreaking onto his considerable body a succession of indentations, curtailments, so that whatever memory of him the townspeople might, if pressed, recuperate later in the light of their houses would be that of an incompletely statured, sideswept man of unfixable purpose. He was not my father (my father had remained unheard of); but because I never addressed him by name (I instead tutoyered him left and right), observers understandably conformed the two of us to their familiar, cleanly notion of father and son.

He would tolerate no footwear under his roof. It was an issue, a policy, of hygiene. He held to a conviction about the unmanageable filthiness of shoes—that once you suffered contact with the bottom of one, you sank to the level of everything the shoe had ever been brought down upon. The piss slopped onto lavatory floors and then tracked everywhere by dint of the retentive sole of a publicly worn slipper was his standard, weary example. And then the house would have the entire clientele of the lavatory circulating throughout it: the house would be thrown wide open again.

The man designed promising clothes.

I adolesced diplomatically by his side. I put in long days in the wide, thorough rooms. My heart *performed*. I fetched whatever the man pointed to. He had a rapid, nominating hand.

I was his head of hair. He would lay claim to the tacky mass of it—redisperse it, superintend it differently, complicate it with ribbons and barrettes, adjust the lights in it, provoke it to fresh successes. I would allow him to have his full say where I was just nerveless, slippery lengths.

In turn, he sought control of the cooking. He plotted our meals with a dismal rigor, mobilizing faded cuts of ham, even paler partings, sectionings, of fruit, jeopardizations of it, along the narrow extent of countertop. (An article of food should present itself as something else, he demanded, arranging lesioned vegetables on a tray for the headboard. "To cool the backs of the knees," he said. Or: "For where your feet will one day have to go.") The days I locked myself in my room, I could count on a raggedness of beef, in sheets, to be slid into thick wallets of bread and then be remitted, relinquished, on the mat outside the door I kneeled behind.

For I had already flung myself into the books that were expected to cause me the most trouble: our sickliest histories. I loitered in them: I stooped on the sentences, bestrode the tensed, buckling words, squatted there until the spread of events became mine alone.

The man knew, too. "What will you use for money?" was how he couched his knowledge.

Our life continued in this train for months. With my ear against the door, I could make out, when I wanted to, the fussing snitter of a scissors or the motory

148

commotions of the sewing machine or, less often, the cantillation, intimate and menial, of the man's telephone voice. (There was a backer he was required to call.) I noticed that a woman from time to time passed by my window: we began to exchange waves. Nothing serious or signific at first—but, before long, a greeterly incontinence took hold of the two of us: our arms shivered away from our sides: even our wristfalls became communicational, *summative*. The first time I climbed all the way out, she guided me to where she said she slept: an ulterior milieu of lotions, spot cash, pedestaled cake savers ajar with the surrounding town. My hands lent themselves to her pink, winking undernesses. (She had the prevailing anatomy.) We made plans to meet again halfway between us. She named some eligible district.

A less penalized course of retrospection, however, would find me having already found that there was a living to be made by furnishing grounds for others in the town to regard me consanguineously: to knock on a door and be shown to a seat and then, by polite, solacing intervals, be drawn out as the furthermost yet of kin. I thus fingered their ashtrays, left informing redolences on their sofas and chairs. I wore a welcome hole in their lives. For once, mothers would have been in the right to talk in secret twos and threes. But how wrong could they have been to keep counting their children on the sly every hour on the hour? When at last the time came to eat, we confronted a speckiness in shallow bowls. Afterward, I would be alternately detested and regaled—the butt of every confidence. I remember setting enough nights aside to compose a hat: an extremely curtained and commemorative number that was later to be accorded that ill-intentioned popularity.

The strings one neglectedly—neglectingly—pulls!

For it was on the strength of this hat alone, the boxed mock-up of it, that I advanced to another man: this one importunate, futureless, adept. We mostly had to travel.

His house and his "finds" (I am free to quote merely from the will) in time demised to me. I had to be driven out for a look at the place. What I could make out had a loose, unmastered aspect in the supplementary light I had been reminded to bring along.

After the auction: prompt, forgivable descents into marriage.

Delora: she must have lived her life in advance of the actual events, because her stomach would accept nothing further. (But she had advantages of height, of moisture.)

Grete: mornings, after shaking out our sheets, she claimed to see "blue minerals" all over the floor. (These she is said to still be sweeping.)

Liann: a whiled-away, vanishing girl. (She had come up through the ranks of her sisters.)

I hope I was impossible.

I hope I told all of them the same thing—that under no circumstances should the body ever have to depict *itself*.

More in keeping, then, with the nature of this anniversary confession are my chances, much later in life, of having had a boy looking in on me after work. (The work was the boy's alone.)

Then the boy fell sick.

The doctor squeezed his, the doctor's, face shut while he, the doctor, spoke terribly of English.

Both of them gave me their money so it would not have to go for food.

Not the Hand but Where the Hand Has Been

People will hold you to your secrets.

So put your finger, for the time being, on a man whose daughter is already grown.

By grown, I mean she no longer lives where I can.

By daughter, I mean she gives off, suffers from, comes down with.

Sometimes I still go where she stays. The bus is more like a waiting room than a corridor, but I am hardly one to sit.

Have I as much as said that, once, an afternoon, I had to ask to use her bathroom, and something turned up, naturally, in the cabinet under the sink? It took me at most a minute or two to get it figured out: it was the fluted plastic rod whose office it is to steady the roll of tissue lengthwise in the toilet-paper holder. But at the time, for the moment, I had it taken for something else. Because it was all by itself down there—set apart, put out. All *treasured*-looking, and privileged. Women, because of how much better they are, or how much better they have it, get to own things—instruments— that men should almost never have to find reason to touch. Even at my age (I have reached my thinning forties), it is a misfortune to be reminded of even where

151

they get stored. But this, for once, was something simpler to put right.

The sound of small things being rearranged has always been, for me, among the hardest to abide. But I remember taking hold of the roll of tissue, working the rod through the cardboard tube, slotting everything into the assembly glued to the pink tile.

"Dad," I heard her say, not even tapping at the door, or at least clittering her fingernails against it, but just barely *patting* the thing. (I swear I could see it move a little in its frame.)

Spare me the spectacle of people fending for themselves.

From early on, it had been a marriage that held no real sway. (Littlenesses, piled high, do not suddenly amount to anything immense.) None of it would even deserve reminiscence if the outfit my wife was working for, a realty, hadn't relocated to a newer building, one that had been rushed up, I'm now guessing, to throw people together. (Sliding glass partitions, everything modular and portable, impermanent.) My wife liked her men noticeably put upon, conspicuously ruined. (He was a title searcher upstairs, I later learned.) For a time, I worked out a compensatory adultery of my own: the source was a woman of immediate physical utility and careful demeanor, a phlebotomist. What we felt for each other lacked any basis in either one of us—it was a hard-nosed tribute, I'm supposing, to people before and yet to come—but we catered to some unrealizable ideal of infidelity and kept up the cattish decencies it called for. Quickly: I was going with her, and then the two of us were going, "together" (her word), with a third, and then there were just the two of them, coupled, professing surprise and self-reproach.

Then I did what I'm still answering for.

Even so, I ask a lot of what I can't see.

If it's a question of looking into a face you haven't run across before and inquiring of yourself just how far it's a corruption of, a judgment on, some other face you are not yet sick of, and then, in the time left (let's insist the two of you are on a bus), doing it some swift, scathing kindnesses—if it's a question, that is, of bestowing upon it an undeserved deprecatory merit—my answer is that my regard for such faces has become almost entirely subtractive, that I do my best to fatigue and deplete their features until the faces go blank and I can thus institute her onto (*found* her looks upon, call her to order on) everybody I see: I put her squarely in my way every place I get.

I mention this because there's a store I can make it to on foot, a drug and grocery combined, where I look at people who are almost never her.

I tack from aisle to aisle, an accumulator. I carry one of the red plastic shopping baskets.

Things between me and the checkout girls could hardly be more tacit. The first of them is reducible to deep hair, a lofty forehead. The second is a bolt of college material fading fast. She twiddles each item she rings up, editorializing with a wry cigarette cough. Everything—grapes, bleach, disposable razors—earns a familiar tussive dismissal. The third is actually a boy (spared so far!), but surely, slenderly, alert that his current body (the lint-white scraps he gets for arms, above all) counts for nothing.

153

Today I get the third girl, the near miss. I watch the thickspread man in front of me set up his homey skyline of cartons and cans on the black span of belt. The things I live on—the chocolate chips, the noodles— sag behind the sleek planes of their packaging. They don't hold up.

It's then I see her enter the store, choose a cart: my eyes and my mouth still secure on her face, though she can barely bring herself to wear the things—the lips bit shut, each green eye sunk, minimized, behind its thick, remedial pane.

We do what we always do: we see each other out.

A voice-activated tape recorder keeps me abreast of most of what gets said in my sleep. I keep the thing on the headboard and listen each morning to the playback. What I hear is beyond the range of speech, but I usually have no trouble making out distinct trains of feeling, burdens, better ways of never knowing what it was that hit me. The most useful method of assorting the sounds, I have discovered, is according to the people they were leveled against—the people who get me to pipe up without my knowledge. The supermarket cashier, for starters, the one temporarily a girl: she has me coming out with an opportune murmuration, very throaty and unlike me. The one with the disapproving cough provokes a hectoring, refutative bark. The tone I take with the wife I had to have is, I think, by and large a steady, reasoning tone. And then there is the one to whom I speak as if through what exactly—a gag? a surgical mask? a hanging of handkerchiefs? It comes out struggled and inspissated. I admire the thickening consistency of it. I can tell it's big talk.

I hear myself out like that, unpersuaded, for the better part of the spring. Then I decide to move into a different, nearby city, a less handy one. Within a week, I am complaining to the building manager about noise from the apartment below mine. The offending tenant is described to me as "a woman away on vacation." The manager grudgingly sympathizes with me for however long it takes the two of us to get to the bottom of the same stairs. From my new address, the commute by bus is fifty-five minutes instead of the accustomed, preoccupied twelve. My career, in fact, breaks up. ("Uncollegiality," "insufficient service to the community," a "fat backlog of name-withheld-by-request grievance letters, for photocopied samples of which please see attached," etc.) A week of busy sleep, and I become an indexer, a freelance. I manufacture indexes for university-press books. I discover I am partial to narrow lanes of type, ragged rights, the appearance given of a settled intelligence. It's private, satisfying work. (A mimeographed pamphlet, a hornbook provided by an editor, describes the ideal indexer as "a person prepared to content herself, minutely and anonymously, with water under the bridge.") I work independently, get paid by the book. The trick is to push your way into the society, or coterie, of facts that the author has pushed his way into first, and then it's a matter of making up your mind to cooperate with what you read. Next, decide on your headings, your *See also*s, and (when appropriate) your subheadings and sub-subheads. As for the rest of the job, who can't handle page numbers? Who can't run the alphabet? (The pamphlet devotes a stocky paragraph to the matter of how easily, given a rogue shove, the "entire works" of a book can be tilted away from the author, or "be made to tick differently," and cautions against the temptation, understandable though rarely understood, for the indexer to take one or more "keynotes," "unheard concerns," of her own life, then fudge them into the run-in, alphabetized biographical arraignment that follows any entry whose headword is a proper name. Other warnings, monitions, mostly concern the treatment of numbers.)

I set my own hours and operate out of my bed. For my off-duty periods (though the pamphlet insists that "an indexer is never not working"), I find it helpful to arrange things around the apartment as prompts, cues. In the bathroom I hang a picture of a woman enjoying a shower (I am otherwise prone to baths that go on too long), in the kitchenette an instructional clipping about a man who saved himself from choking. Early one morning, I am tipped backward in the dentist's chair for a cleaning. The hygienist is new to me: tall, unquiet, not too removed from herself. From a laminated ID card pinned to her waist I learn her name in full. She presents me with a suave handout about gum sicknesses and a packet of hooklike floss threaders for my bridge. Afterward, up they go on the wall above my bed.

Weeks pass: a book every two days or three. (The pamphlet reassures me that it is not unbecoming for an indexer to perform with such dispatch.) I start skipping the recommended three-by-five cards, the shoe boxes, the colored pencils. I do the alphabetizing on plain loose-leaf, then press the results into the dirty pica of my manual typewriter. (The hollows of the *o*'s come out shaded.)

The stream of my bathroom-sink faucet, I notice, gets thinner and thinner. I come to rely on the faucet of the tub for the water I splash into my eyes. I take down the picture of the showering woman and substitute a newspaper cutting about the problem of getting to sleep and the problem of knowing what needs to be done once you get there.

The second time I eat with the dental hygienist, a new fact (according to her, the simple reason you forget the things that come to you in the middle of the night— the things you think up and regard as yours to carry along into the day ahead—is that the next regime of sleep comes and demands them back) mixes itself in with older ones (her brother's freezer isn't freezing anything, just keeping things soft and damp; she sat on her aunt's deathbed, just a corner of it) and begins to lose some of its narrow value. People have children, she is already saying, to export themselves into the future, which on the face of it I know to be false.

"How many have you got?" she says.

I develop a small following among the local editors, referrals are made, I get asked to do this book and that one. For instance, a man gets around to jerking out a little history of labor unions. The call comes. Within the hour, I have picked up the galleys, begun my dingy involvement. To the hygienist, at my side in bed, I let slip the remark that one instant your life is a complete, if hard-to-see, accumulation of people and all the wrong ideas about them, and then you're already halfway through the next, garnering moment. (The limited light from the lamplet puddling on her bare leg. The unprevented oppression of her hand on my arm as I write down a page number. My tender reminder that there are ways to keep to oneself that do not entail reaching one's full length in bed.)

She is so pleased with herself for having told off the receptionist at work that she repeats the speech in its belated entirety, working wonders with a rich, accusative *you*. My preferred way of being addressed: directly, but as a substitute.

More weeks. (Mornings that get going as if by levers, pulleys; then movement with confidence through the long, paraded hours.) Returning one evening from a walk, I find a paper towel balled up (messagefully?) outside my door. I carry it inside, unwad it, run my eyes over its receptive cellular surface, discover no lip-smears, discolorings, notations, desquamations, gouts of mucus, modest holdings of crumbs or dirt. No communication of even the dustiest, most negligible sort. So I desert the towel on an end table. The moon at my window is glib and complete. The hygienist no longer answers her phone. I go back to baths. I find a way—transparent plastic report covers that slide over the pages, grease pencils, etc.—to bring my work along with me into the tub. My naps, when I start taking them again, are adversarial and to the point. (I come out of them cleared.) A not unforeseen sloppiness, a retaliatory inattention, eventually finds its entrance into my work. I get a call from the editor of the labor-union book. "Can you take criticism?" she says. ("As I believe I told you..." is how I have come to initiate all responses.) On the bus down, I watch a man busy himself with a snug, compatible rubber band. On the bus back, I open the folder, squint through the boscage of green question marks that shoot up at me from every page, and read what I remember having submitted:

"other crannies," 00; excuse for recumbency ("Just resting my heart"), 00; "faraway powder room" of, 00; fastenings of, 00; feeling of being walked rather than of walking, 00; first swing taken at parents of, 00; footage of yellowed foam rubber on which she sometimes drowsed, 00; forms of greeting, 00; on the "fresh disappointments in the way things look from one instant to the next," 00; game made of sitting in chair still keeping the heat of, 00; as "gazingstock," 00; glassy, almost transpicuous incisor of (unsuccessful attempt to inspect untrimmed arclet of fingernail through), 00; "grabbiness" of, 00; handbag, inventory of contents of, 00; handholds, footsteps, stays, 00; on having the air blow right over her, 00; and the "heart's chores," 00; heavy lifting and, 00; heyday of, 00; on "how good I am getting at sponging mouth-marks off the glasses," 00; on how the strip of cellophane tape captured dust and hair on the way to the page waiting to be mended (volutions of the fingerprint grimily visible in the face of the tape), 00; on how things upstairs sounded to people underneath (creak from each footfall rippling outward until it overspread the entire ceiling of the room, the resultant effect one of "accomplishment"), 00; "huttish" characteristics of bedroom of, 00; "I have always had the best reason in the world to be afraid of my own shadow: it's of me," 00; idea for a book printed on paper specially treated and weighted so that when the book was removed from the display and browsed through, the book always fell open to the same page, 00; on the "importance" of furniture ("It elevates you"), 00; on "the incidental, auxiliary violence one might do to what has already been done," 00; "inconsolably okay," 00; insistence that "all the words available to me have already gone through too many mouths—all come out meaning the same thing," 00; "insomniac eminence" of, 00; intercrural entertainments with, 00; intervening decades of, 00; "Is it one mistake after another, or is it the same one divvied up to make it last from one day to the next?," 00; judged to be visitable, 00; kitchen of, lit by pilot lights, 00;

human anatomy mistaken for map, 00; procedure for dividing room into "quadrants," 00; proposed elevated footway for, 00; puberulent surfaces of, 00; ragweed season and, 00; "rained-on" smell of inner bend of elbow of, 00; readerly behavior of (tendency to drift to the horizon of the page), 00; records of acne of, found (atlaslike notebook, a double page for each day, on the verso an oval representing the left hemisphere of her face, circles representing pimples; recto showing right hemisphere; legend at bottom explaining system of shading and cross-hatching devised to indicate stages in growth cycle of each pustule ["emerging," "peaking," "receding"], everything done in faint pencilry; "like page after page of star charts"), 00; remark that "the opposite of saying something still involves making way too much noise," 00; on the "responsibility of taking on an appearance," 00; "roof falling in on," 00; room of (tenpenny nail protruding from wall at eye level of, resultless attempts to extract the nail, the window envelope thus impaled upon it as a

warning), 00; "rug pulled out from under," 00; on running into people met during former educations, 00; saying good-bye before shutting the door for a bath, 00; "scenic cosmeticism" of face of, 00; seat cushion of, 00; "self-eclipsing" manner of entering a room, 00; self-spectatorship and, 00; sheltering car of, 00; "shingled heartwreck" of a house of, 00; shower-curtain pattern, 00; shown to have typing ability, 00; sightlines of, from bed and desk chair, 00; on sinking one's heart into, 00; in slacks, 00; as sneak, 00; soilures of, 00; "speaking against the language," 00; spoken ill of, 00; "spurning bed" of, 00; as stacker, boxer, bagger, shelver, 00; status of neck of, 00; storm-felled tree branches compared, playfully, to antlers, 00; stretch of wall between hamper and dresser of, 00; subclothes of, 00; at table, 00; taking the sun, 00; telephone as a "calamity of black plastic," 00; telephone, misdescription of the "strainer" of the "talk cup," 00; telephone personality of, 00; temptation to concede that "the world sorts itself out into people stuck to their stories and people walking scantly up the stairs to put out," 00; tendency to be hard on people the second time they are run across on any given day, 00; tendency to pick up an object by introducing a paper towel between the object and the receiving hand, 00; as tireless obliterator of the hours before bed, 00; toiletries preferred by, 00; town, low-roofed, untrafficable in the heat, 00; trouble with her dreams (their having been obviously, insultingly, intended for somebody else; their having arrived in her sleep after being turned away by other people; their never including any of her belongings), 00; trouble with throwing things out (there not being a sense of anyone on the receiving end acknowledging the arrival of any particular piece of garbage, the desire for the process of disposal to be a "requited act," for things not so much to disappear as to be "put in the way of" somebody else, the necessity for such a person to know what was someone else's at some point, reassurance of something's having changed

hands, etc.), 00; in the tub, 00; "underhouse," tablet sketchings of, 00; unnaming the dog of, steps involved in, 00; on "the unseen world as an apology for the seen," 00; venation of (face and neck), 00; verification that "it starts when you discover that you can keep yourself at arm's length: you practice conducting your life at farther and farther reaches from the body—except you do not want to be allowed any longer to get away with calling it a body (which would be an arrogance) and insist instead on being required to regard it at most as a *steadiment*: the station, that is, which the heart, the mouth, the eyes, etc., can be said (variously) to occupy, to be the 'guest' of, or to trespass upon," 00; visitor book discovered, 00; voice of, said to "desert" the mouth, 00; "The well-made bed is always fuller of discoveries than the blowzy one," 00; "Whatever you eat, just make sure you look it over real good before you eat it," 00; where found, 00; "wide, booming floor" of, 00; window coverings sought by, 00

I get myself roped into further jobs: product assembler, loss preventer, Clerk Typist II. The way the other passengers on the bus keep bringing up what they had for lunch in thrifty, time-killing esophageal aftersurges, I discover, by accident, that I can fetch the tastes, the flavors, of things I once ate at her side, things we swallowed together when she was still in school. I become a specialist in summoning the tang of cheap, bygone candy. I bring the taste back, release it from what has long been claiming it, then waft it out of my mouth and into the already spoiled air. I accomplish this extramolecularly and with a contempt for whatever minimal biology it requires. People—for some reason men, especially—sense what I am up to, take a liking to what they are inhaling, reseat themselves by hopeful, discreet stages. Before the bus reaches their stops, some of the men ask me to spit onto little scrips of newspaper, which are then folded and secluded into sports-jacket pockets, for later. One afternoon, a man who has taken the seat next to mine starts thinking aloud about how long he has set store by a waxen variety of hollow chocolate, with a stalish pallor, or bloom, all over it—and I remember a marked-down, end-of-season bunny I bought her one year, and I bring the far-off, hushaby savor of the chocolate up into the trough of my mouth and fit my lips punctually, resuscitatively, onto his.